The Long Climb Back

by Jill L Hicks

Dear Robin,
I hope you
enjoy the journey!
Blessings,
Jill Hicks

This book is a work of fiction. Names, characters, businesses, organizations, places, events, and incidents either are the product of the author's imagination or are used fictitiously. Any resemblance to actual persons, living or dead, or events is entirely coincidental.

Cover photograph and design by Bill Hicks

12/27/13

This book is dedicated to my sisters and brother
Judy Martin
Joan Yarnall
Joyce Abel
Jane Niven
Randy Yarnall Jr.

What a great trip it has been!

THE LONG CLIMB BACK

A canyon, by definition, is a deep chasm impossible to span in a large step or leap. Such foolishness would subject one to serious injury or even death. I have contemplated this outcome at great length. While attractive to the eye with its rock formations, fragile vegetation, and various species of wildlife, canyons can be treacherous to traverse. Most canyons were carved into the earth by the brutal force of raging water and weather related extremes. That same capacity is evident in the rivers and streams that continue to run through them while providing picturesque scenery. Created in violence, they continue to evolve with the coexistence of awe-inspiring beauty and dangerous savagery.

When I look at canyon walls, history shouts at me. It is very loud.

CHAPTER ONE

ANGELICA

I couldn't wait to board that plane. I needed a week of solitude away from my fiancé, our families, and his family's business. Everything had been moving way too fast for my comfort.

Mathieu and I had been dating for a little over three months when he popped the question. His proposal came much sooner than I had anticipated. I had given thought to the eventual possibility, but Mathieu and I had never shared a serious conversation prior to his over-the-top proposal. It was the last thing I had expected from a man who was all about personal success and calculated risks.

At the time, I could not have told you if he wanted children, and if so, how many? Did he want to continue to live in his rural countryside estate, or would we build a new home of our own? What about his spiritual life? Did he believe in anything other than himself and his family's enterprises? To what political party did he subscribe? His chronic chivalrous behavior led me to believe that he was a conservative, but social graces and politics do not always go hand-in-hand.

Most importantly, and second only to children, did Mathieu want a dog? If he was allergic to dogs, or just flat out did not want one or two, we would have a problem. Would he be amenable to a rescue dog? Or, would it have to be some sort of exotic breed?

The one thing that I had learned in our short time together was that family status and reputation were very important to Mathieu and his parents. It was easy for me to spot because my own parents lived by the same creeds. Trying desperately to define myself, it was something that I had struggled with as a young adult.

I had to respond to his proposal in front of his parents, my parents, a pilot, and a videographer. What else could I have said? I loved him enough that I did not want to hurt or embarrass him. He had gone through great lengths to set up the extravagant event. Everything with Mathieu had to be larger than life. Sometimes, I thought his only daily aim was to overwhelm me. He was highly successful in his endeavors, which was not always necessarily good. After his proposal, I was beginning to feel the accumulated effects of a few miscalculations he had made along the way in our very young relationship.

Mathieu was an only child, and so was I. Along with our families' fortunes, it was another thing we had in common. We shared the pressures that came with the intense adoration of our intrusive yet well-meaning parents. There were no other siblings to help us diffuse their focused attention. There was no one to run interference when we needed it. We were obligated to include our families in each and every personal and monumental event.

It was my twenty-sixth birthday, and Mathieu wanted to surprise me with something I had never done before - hot air ballooning. He picked me up at 5:00 PM and we drove an hour southwest to a large field in Cecil County, Maryland. The pilot, ground crew, videographer, and both sets of parents were waiting there to greet us. More to my shock and silent horror, a film crew and its helicopter were on stand-by about 100 yards away from the intended lift-off site. It was all adding up to another one of Mathieu's big productions.

Earlier in the day, Mathieu had called to say that one of his couriers would be delivering several packages to my home and to make sure I received them before he picked me up for our date that evening.

"I think you're going to love what I have in mind. And Angelica, pull your hair up; it might be a little breezy. I love you, Angel. Always and forever."

A simple birthday cake, a few kisses, maybe a small piece of jewelry, or flowers would have been nice enough for me.

Mathieu's courier arrived within the hour and handed the first box over to my roommate, Camille.

Camille and I had met in college where we became fast friends. Once we graduated, we moved back to my hometown where my parents purchased a large house for us to call home. They called it an investment. I believed it was another one of their schemes to keep me under their tight scrutiny. My parents loved Camille and were immediately pleased when I announced that she was moving in with me.

"Oooo, Angie! Your fabulously rich boyfriend has sent you a birthday present from Ophelia's Studio! (Ophelia's was one of the top fashion design houses in New York City.)

"Open it! Open it!" Camille squealed. She was always more excited than I was about the various packages Mathieu would send. She claimed that she was living vicariously through me. Sometimes, I thought Mathieu and Camille would have made the perfect couple. But, for the time being, I wanted to live the dream.

The designer box was secured shut with a two inch pink silk ribbon and capped off with a bow that was fashioned into a rose. The first several times Mathieu sent extravagant gifts, I could not figure out how to open the packages without destroying their elegant wrappings. I called my mother. She would know the proper way to handle such ostentatious accoutrements.

"Just cut the damn ribbon, Angie. The bows are inconsequential to the gift inside. That's what really counts."

My father had sent my mother expensive gifts with excessive wrapping on many occasions during their thirty plus years of history together. I later learned that it meant he was in some kind of trouble and that he was trying to buy his way out of solitary confinement. Already over the top, I could not imagine what tactics Mathieu would employ if he ever needed to regain my good graces.

Inside the box was an envelope addressed to me. I lifted it out of the box, broke the personalized seal on the back, and pulled out the note.

"My Dear Angel,
Happy Birthday!
Please grace your beautiful body with these garments designed with you in mind. While nothing compares or deserves to be draped upon you soft shoulders, I cannot have you soaring above the countryside naked. We can soar naked later. That's if you'll have me.
I will pick you up at 5:00 PM.
I love you,
Always and forever,
Mathieu"

Inside the box and wrapped in ornate tissue, I found a breezy chiffon top. Its pastel floral pattern was constructed in several layers and lined with a body hugging bra-top camisole. I had never shared my actual size with Mathieu, but his personal shopper always got it right - 36C. Below the top, and wrapped in the same tissue, was a pair of white cotton/spandex capris, size 4. Tucked below all the tissue was a linen envelope inscribed with my initials. Inside the envelope was a white lace thong, of course.

There was another knock on the door. Camille, still googly-eyed by the first parcel, rushed to greet the deliveryman.

"Special delivery for Angelica Havens."

"I can sign for that, I'm her roommate."

I heard the door slam shut and Camille scamper into our spacious living area carrying two shoe-sized boxes. Sure enough a pair of Nora sandals and a small matching shoulder bag were included to complete the perfect ensemble.

"How does one land a guy like Mathieu Dufour?" Camille would always ask.

Mathieu's limo pulled up in front of my house at exactly 5:00. Donald, his driver, stepped out and opened the back passenger door. Mathieu slipped out and waited for me by his oversized SUV.

"Oh. My. God. Angie, wait until you get a load of your man. Jeez, he is so hot." Camille was always excited to see Mathieu. If I did not know better, I would have said just the sight of him melted her core. Actually, I did know better, and yes, he did have that effect on her. However, I could not fault her for a very natural reaction to his exceptionally good looks.

I grabbed my new shoulder bag, hugged Camille on the way out, and exited through the front door. Camille was not exaggerating. Mathieu was dressed in a white linen shirt. His untucked tails were blowing in the slight breeze providing glimpses his rock-hard tanned torso. He was leaning back against the car with his hands tucked into the pockets of his jeans. When he saw me, he stood erect and strolled toward me with his arms wide open. His unruly hair always completed his youthful bad-boy look. His deep blue eyes, almost navy, never left mine as he lifted me into his embrace and gently placed a soft kiss on my lips.

"Happy Birthday, Beautiful!" he whispered somewhere into my hair. He stepped back and twirled me around to examine his purchase. "Very nice. Perfect for what I have in mind for you this evening. Come."

Mathieu took my hand and escorted me to the Lincoln. Standing by, Donald held the door open for us.

"Miss Havens, you look lovely this evening," Donald remarked.

"I bet you say that to all the girls, Donald."

"None of them were named Miss Angelica Havens," he winked.

I clutched before stepping into the Lincoln. Donald broke a smile. He was always the kidder and kept me on my toes.

I laughed and shook my head at him.

"And, none have been as beautiful as you, Miss Havens," he added, flashing his usual comedic smile. As he closed the door, I could see that he was pleased with his jest.

"Ignore him," Mathieu chided as he slid his arm around my shoulders.

Donald drove us to a vast open field where a giant hot air balloon was coming to life. A large fan blew fiery heat from its burners and into the mouth of the colorful airship that would eventually carry us heavenward. The fabric began to billow and roll. The motor of the fan combined with the thrusts from the burners was loud and made a harsh sound that forced us to speak to one another in raised decibels. Standing by the SUV, we were greeted and joined by the pilot, Mathieu's parents, and mine. I had no clue that Mom and Dad were going to be there; that was part of the surprise. I noticed that my dad seemed a little on edge. My mother was going on like a chatterbox. It was a sure sign that she was nervous about something.

Mathieu hugged me around my waist and pointed out what each crewmember was doing. It seemed he had done this before. Trying to maintain control, the ground crew pulled back on the balloon's lines when it started filling out, taking shape, and rising off the ground. "Dufour Winery & Distributors" was clearly imprinted around its largest area of circumference. A grape vine pattern danced above, below, and through the letters. It was a sight to see, and it was obvious the Dufour family hoped that many would.

"Who's going up?" I asked. I was curious as to how much weight we were going to load into the craft's wicker basket, which was still on its side.

"You, me, our parents, and the videographer."

I probably looked puzzled by the seemingly large crowd Mathieu had invited along for the ride. Mathieu casually claimed that the basket could easily carry eight people.

"Wait here!" he yelled over top of the fan motor and burner blasts. He left my side and joined the crew at the tail of a long heavy line connected to the top of the balloon. It looked like a great game of tug-of-war, which I knew the balloon would eventually win as it expanded and rose up. The videographer quickly gathered his equipment to film Mathieu working alongside the crew. When the balloon tugged, the crew and Mathieu dug their heels into the ground, their shoulders strained, and their biceps bulged as they pulled back on the line.

As expected, all of the crewmembers were extremely good-looking. The Dufours surrounded themselves with handsome men and beautiful women. Because of that prerequisite, I had trouble understanding how I fit into their carefully crafted puzzle. I must have been their trophy that said they could mingle with, and even love, the commoner. Camille debated my rationale fiercely.

"First, your family is rolling in dough; otherwise, we wouldn't be living in a place like this. Second, look at you! You're gorgeous and built like a Victoria's Secret Angel."

Camille had a habit of exaggerating, especially when it came to boosting my spirits. It was one of the many reasons why I loved her.

The pilot nodded when the balloon was fully inflated and boasting all of its glorious colors to the world. On cue, the crew released the top tether, and the fan was shut down. Our surroundings quieted with the exception of the burners occasionally breathing fire and the click-hum of camera shutters.

The large wicker basket stood up and revealed a door that would let us in. However, that also meant it had a door that could let us out mid-flight. I silently vowed that once we were aloft I would stay away from that door.

With everyone onboard, the pilot, who Mathieu introduced as "Captain Henri Harding," covered a list of safety instructions for our launch, flight, and eventual landing. Secretly, I was already looking forward to our safe return to earth.

"It's nothing more than a controlled crash," Captain Harding quipped about the landing. Everyone, except me, appreciated his humor. I felt good about the captain's confidence, but his statement did nothing to calm my fears. *Sometimes it's best to temper the truth.* Then he asked if there were any questions. There were none.

"Mathieu, are you ready to go?" the Captain asked.

Mathieu looked at me and then replied, "I have never been more ready in my life." Mathieu looked down at me once more, and I saw intense longing in his eyes. It was the kind of longing I had seen behind his closed doors. *Not now, Mathieu.* He tightened his grip on me, but I was too nervous to reciprocate his affection. *Don't hold on so tight; I need to breathe and keep my balance here.*

Captain Harding opened the burners. A long blast of fire began filling the cavernous space above our heads with intense heat. Standing in the basket, I could feel the tension between the air temperature outside and the overheated air inside the expanded cloth structure above us. Something had to give. *Oh my God, this is it!* I prayed no one noticed my shaking knees and shortness of breath. I had an acute fear of heights. Apparently, Mathieu did not know that about me, and it was obvious that my parents had not mentioned it to him when he made the arrangements for my over-the-top birthday present.

To my surprise, after the crew released the basket we quickly began our ascent and rose straight up into the sky. Before I could consider our climbing speed and rising altitude, the beauty of the countryside below overcame me. The hues of lush green trees and pastures, plus the dimensions of the landscape now accentuated by long evening shadows, rolling hills, rivers, and streams all served to put my anxiety at rest. Exhilarated by the quick launch and the spread of vistas laid out below us, I hugged

Mathieu and he kissed me in front of everyone. I was keenly aware that our videographer was focused in on us. Laying his lips against my ear, he whispered, "I love you, Angelica Orabelle Havens, always and forever."

Rarely, did anyone call me by my full name. First, I didn't offer it up unless it was required. Second, it almost always compelled me to give an explanation for my unique middle name. "Orabelle" was my maternal grandmother's first name. It means "beautiful seacoast." My grandmother went by "Belle," which was completely understandable. Third, my close friends called me "Angie." However, Mathieu's family had a thing for formalities. His parents always called their son, Mathieu, never Matt. Early on in our relationship, they made sure I knew the correct spelling of his formal name. Heaven forbid I should get it wrong for the press or any form of documentation.

On our first official date, Mathieu told me that "Angie" did not properly convey the sophisticated elegance he saw in me. So, "Angelica" and "Angel" became the terms of endearment that Mathieu adopted. I had grown accustomed to them in our three short months together.

As we soared above the countryside, Mathieu and Captain Harding directed our attention to various points of interest. Looking behind us, the Northeast River glowed like a bright silver strand as it drifted south to the head of the Chesapeake Bay where it met up with the Susquehanna and Elk Rivers. Heading northeast, we soon crossed into Pennsylvania. Large farms created a patchwork quilt seamed together by fences and linear-move irrigation systems. One particular farm sported an outdoor riding ring. It looked as if someone had painted a large geometric figure known as a "stadium" on the ground. Adjacent to the outdoor ring was a massive indoor arena. Its red roof and tan wood exterior provided a striking contrast to the green fields surrounding it. In a large pasture, several dozen horses grazed lazily. Concerned about the unfamiliar object approaching their airspace above the earth, we occasionally heard dogs barking as they attempted to alert their people of the possible advancing threat. Aside from the dogs and the intermittent blast of fired heat from the burners, we sailed silently across the sky. The bucolic setting of Southern Chester County was breathtaking to say the least.

US Route 1 was easy to spot as were the large vineyards owned by Mathieu's family. The rows and rows of grapevines outlined the contours of the endless estate with long running parallel lines that trouped across its hilltops and dove into its valleys. Even from aloft, The Dufour Vineyard was pristine. Our altitude failed to diminish the size of the winery's barn. It still appeared warm and majestic. It was a sight to see the shadow of the giant Dufour Winery hot air balloon glide over its namesake. That's when Mathieu reached down and opened a small cooler his father had carried onboard. My attention was drawn back to things of closer proximity. I saw my mother take a deep breath and hold her hands to her chest. It was another give away that something was up, but what happened next I could not have predicted. From a distance, I heard a helicopter fast approaching. It was the very same aircraft that was stationed in the field from which we had launched.

"I think it's time for a little champagne," Mathieu announced proudly as he pulled flutes from the cooler and began distributing them among his guests. "Dufour Winery & Distributors" was etched into the thin crystal and matched the logo on the hot air balloon. Then he reached for a bottle, and with the smooth expertise of a sommelier, Mathieu popped the cork and sent it flying over Southern Chester County. He held the open bottle over the side of the basket allowing the escaping bubbly to vaporize over the countryside below. I heard his father snap a picture. Mathieu turned the bottle carefully, got down on one knee, and held the label up to me.

Is he asking me to approve the vintage? Oh, I hope not. I know very little about wines, especially compared to the collective knowledge of my present company.

It was very intimidating. His father snapped off several more pictures. Captain Harding pretended nothing was out of the ordinary. I had never seen champagne served in that way, and I did not know what to do.

"Sure, that would be very nice," seemed the proper response. I held my glass down toward Mathieu's lowered stature. He pushed the bottle a little closer toward me. Then, I saw it. The gold embossed label read:

"Angelica Orabelle Havens,
Will you please marry me?
I love you,
Always and forever,
Mathieu Olivier Dufour"

"What?"

I am sure that was not the first response Mathieu was expecting to hear, nor was the next.

"Do you know what this says?" I frantically questioned him and pointed toward the bottle in his hand. That was when I noticed the diamond ring secured to the neck of the bottle by a thin gold chain.

"Of course, I know what it says. I wrote it! What do you say?" Mathieu looked up at me through his dark boyish lashes. He appeared so uncharacteristically vulnerable.

The helicopter was circling the balloon at a dizzying rate of speed. Frazzled, my mind raced.

Is this the fairy-tale proposal my girlfriends and I had fantasized about? Or, is this a publicity stunt? Is he serious? Of course he is. Look at him. Did my parents know about this?

I looked over to my mother and father. They did not appear to be in shock. They were impatiently waiting for my answer. They knew. I looked over at Mathieu's mother. Unfortunately, I had never mastered how to read her always-inscrutable face. His father gave me his classic one-sided smile, a Dufour family trait.

"Angel, you're killing me here. Will you please marry me?" Mathieu whispered. Never had he looked so defenseless. I could tell the wait was making him squirm with apprehension. He was not familiar with the feeling of helplessness and was failing miserably to hide it.

I cannot stand to see a child struggle or an animal suffer. I will do what ever it takes to put an end to their distress. Yes, I am that girl. So, I really did not give much thought to my answer. It was more of a reaction to eliminate Mathieu's deep discomfort.

"Yes. Of course, I will."

There, the moment I had waited for all my life was over. In the pop of a champagne cork and a fancy label presented in a floating billboard, my life took a swift ninety-degree turn and veered away from the course I had aptly set for the past twenty-six years.

The champagne flowed. Captain Harding abstained stating that he would celebrate with us once we landed, or should I say, successfully executed our controlled crash. Boasting that they had known all along, our parents congratulated us and acknowledged that it was a perfect match made in heaven. *How ironic.* Suddenly, it became painfully obvious to me that my decision was never really mine to make.

Mathieu Olivier Dufour could not have been happier. He had pulled it off. Standing up, he pulled me into his six-foot frame and kissed me long and hard while our fathers snapped pictures. The videographer kept his camera aimed at us, and the helicopter circled several more times. Champagne flutes were filled, toasts were made, none of which I remember, and various poses were requested and struck for the cameras. I was being swept away and everything was perfectly out of control with the exception of our able captain and his airship, thank God.

What just happened? I admired the ring now on my finger. *This is for real. I just committed to spend the rest of my life with this man, someone I had only known for three short months.*

I could feel my chest drawing tight. Though I was sky high and surrounded by a great expanse of the clear blue, I needed more air. I needed to get away to think about what I had just done. My eyes were glazing over, and voices turned to muffled bursts of sound. *Don't hyperventilate, not here, not now.* I was trapped a thousand feet above the earth with nowhere to go. The burners continued to blast randomly as the helicopter finally disappeared into the horizon. I would have to tough it out until my feet were back on solid ground.

It was no surprise that my parents adored Mathieu. Both families must have been scheming together when they had arranged our first meeting. Our fathers belonged to and played golf together at the very prestigious Pine Valley Golf Club. One Sunday afternoon, which was the only day women were permitted on the course, our fathers took Mathieu and me out for a friendly foursome.

I can play as well as any of the guys, and when driving from the ladies' tee, I can be a real threat. I'm not boasting. It is just a statement of fact. I have the signed scorecards and records that substantiate my claims.

Mathieu watched as I blasted my first drive straight up the fairway and landed closest to the green. I birdied the first hole. My dad grinned, Mr. Dufour swore, and Mathieu leaned handsomely on his putter admiring my first sink of the day.

"And that's how it's done," I said to myself. *"This is going to be a good day. A good day, indeed."*

Mathieu was great company that entire afternoon. He complimented my swings, laughed when he hit the sand trap, and he eventually ended up driving my cart that was once occupied by my father. I'm not sure how it happened, but it really did not matter. I enjoyed sharing the ride time with Mathieu on the back nine. Not only was he a charming gentleman, Mathieu was easy on the eyes. His thick jet-black hair curled out from under his baseball cap. His European tan added to his playful outdoorsy look. His dark eyes were an amazing navy blue framed by long lashes.

They gave him the appearance of an innocent soul. The one-sided smile that he inherited from his father added dark and dangerous undertones to his sex appeal. After spending a year in the south of France, he had recently returned stateside. It sounded as though he may have picked up a bit of an accent while there. Admittedly, I enjoyed watching his broad shoulders come around his narrow hips as he drove the ball and tried to match or better the lie of my own. If he liked his drive, his eyes would follow the ball, and then he would pump his driver. If he was disappointed, he would look away, take a one-arm swing through the air with his driver, pick up his tee, and move on. Mathieu was playful, but only to one end, that it helped him reach his ultimate goal. I soon learned that part of his family's success was built on intense focus and a wicked competitive streak that ran deep, but was concealed from the public for the most part.

Three months later, I accepted Mathieu's proposal a thousand feet above the earth with our meddling, yet well-meaning, parents onboard... literally and figuratively.

MATHIEU

She said, "Yes."
She has agreed to be my bride.
I am the luckiest!

CHAPTER TWO

JARED

"It's going to be the trip of a lifetime!" I called out to my younger brother, Jarvis, who was feverishly packing in the other room.

The house was abuzz with anxious energy as Jarvis prepared for our Grand Circle Tour. My mother had put together a list of everything he needed.

"Layers." That's what Mom said. "Pack in layers. It will be cold at night and hot during the day."

She had done her homework, that's for sure. She always did. Our mother was a single parent who did her best to raise my brother and me, but it was time for her to let go.

"I'm still not convinced this is such a good idea," she muttered under her breath when I arrived at the house the day before our scheduled flight.

Jarvis and I were alike in some ways and very different in others. I was older, much older, and taller, too. I was thirty-one years old and five feet ten inches tall. Jarvis was twenty-two and just shy of five feet nine inches tall. We both had brown hair and brown eyes. I was the athletic one, and Jarvis was the brains of the operation. Mom always said I was the socialite of the family. I guess compared to Jarvis that would be correct, but only because Jarvis was socially impaired. (Mom disliked it when I used the word "impaired.") By the time Jarvis hit the second grade and I was in eleventh and preparing to leave for college, Mom and I had figured out that Jarvis was indeed different. Thankfully, his teachers recognized his "condition" (Mom hated that reference, too) and encouraged us to seek help. However, the school district would not concede to what we already knew until he "passed" a bunch of tests. ("Passed" was a funny word to use when considering what they were actually trying to measure.) Anyway, based on the results of his tests things began to change, and we began the journey of learning how to live in the different world Jarvis occupied under the same roof the three of us shared.

Jarvis had many obsessions. (Mom preferred to call them unique traits.) At the top of the list was his stand-offish-ness. He avoided all visual and physical contact. If and when he talked to you, Jarvis would never look you in the eye. He hated to be touched, and he was hypersensitive to loud noises. When he was younger, he would haul off and pound you if you so much as nudged him, even if you were pushing him away from a speeding car. I can't tell you how many times he had tried to wallop me. Mom claimed that I used to touch him just to start a rumble. I don't really remember that, but it is believable. To this day, when Mom is not around, he will still take a few swings at me just for good measure.

Then there was his need to keep everything in order. Jarvis's bed had to be facing true north. Every night he would look for the North Star to make sure everything was aligned. On cloudy nights, Jarvis would check a compass that Mom had purchased for him to avoid a pointless confrontation. Jarvis made his bed every morning before he left his room. His shoes were lined up perfectly at the foot of his bed. His shirts were organized by color in his closet. When Jarvis got dressed in the morning, or before leaving the bathroom, the front placket of his shirt, his belt buckle, and his fly had to be lined up perfectly. We later learned that the military called this uniform rule a "gig line." In that case, Jarvis thought that he might like to join the military. Mom said an emphatic, "No!" God forbid anything was out of place on his dresser or on his shelves. All of his textbooks were arranged in alphabetical order by author. The currency in his wallet was in order of value, smallest to greatest, and the bills were always faced the same way.

As he grew older, Jarvis became more rigid about his rituals. I began to realize that these regimens were very important to him, and they had to be addressed before he could move on. So, when I was with him, I tried to do my best to walk his straight and narrow. Failing to do so always had its consequences, especially for our mother. Numerous times he had embarrassed us, particularly in restaurants and movie theaters. When he threw tantrums or acted disrespectful, people would look at my mom as if she was the worst parent ever for letting him behave the way he did. When Jarvis first started acting out in public, I would fall behind just so I could confirm the expected grumblings of passers-by. I felt sorry for my mom. I felt sorry for Jarvis, and I felt guilty.

I could have been Jarvis.

JARVIS

Our plane was scheduled to depart Philadelphia International Airport at 7:37 AM, Terminal B, Gate B8. That meant we had to arrive at Gate B8 by 6:37 AM. We had to leave our house by 5:07 AM. Jared said that once we checked in I could get an Auntie Anne's soft pretzel and a Starbuck's mocha latte. Auntie Anne's were my favorite. My mother did not allow me to eat them, or drink coffee. Jared said Mom did not need to know about everything. Jared can be wrong about many things.

I set my alarm for 4:37 AM. I packed everything that I would need for the next 14 days in my duffle bag. I checked each item off the list as I folded and placed it in its proper compartment. Mom wrote down exactly how many boxer briefs, shorts, pants, short sleeve shirts, and long sleeve shirts I would need. She even wrote down the number of socks, and what shoes and jackets to take. She said I had to pack my own duffle bag, but she wrote everything down for me. Sometimes, she treats me like a baby. I am not a baby. I am 22 years, 1 month, and 15 days old. That's 8,080 days.

Jared said our trip would do me good. Jared may be 8 years, 8 months, and 2 days older than me, but he is wrong about many things. Let me tell you how wrong Jared can be.

Jared was married on February 2, 2002. He married Erin Leigh McCann. She liked that date so she could say that she was married on triple deuces: 02/02/02. Erin Leigh McCann thought she was brilliant. She was not. Jared and Erin Leigh McCann were married for 7 years, 2 months, and 18 days. That's 2,634 days. Jared said it was 2,634 days of pure hell. (I told Jared how many days they were married. Jared told me it was pure hell.) Jared can be funny sometimes. Jared was officially divorced on my 21st birthday, April 20, 2009. Happy Birthday to me! We celebrated 2 events that night.

Mom said we would be sleeping in cabins, but I did not see a sleeping bag on her list. I ran downstairs to ask her.

"Mom! A sleeping bag is not on your list. I don't own a sleeping bag! I need to go get a sleeping bag," I informed her.

"No, dear, the cabins have beds and they will have sheets and blankets already made up for you."

She did not hear me.

"We are staying in cabins. We will need sleeping bags," I told her a second time. I usually had to tell her things twice.

"No, the cabins will have beds like a hotel room. You are not camping, and you will not need sleeping bags. It will be like staying in a hotel."

She was not going to change her mind. She was on the phone with someone. She waved me off.

"Flashlights, Mom! Flashlights!" I knew she had forgotten something.

She held the phone away from her mouth. "Good call. Go ahead and pack one." Mom put her hand on my shoulder and pointed me toward the stairs. I hated when she did that. My high school P.E. teacher did that once, and I thought about taking him out. I gave it a good try, too. It landed me in the principal's office. My mom had to drive me home that day. Jared said I should let him know if a teacher ever touched me again. Jared said he would always take care of me. He was wrong about that, too.

I went back upstairs to my room. *No sleeping bags. No sleeping bags. No sleeping bags.*

My favorite pack of number cards was lying on my bed. I had had them since I was in the fourth grade. I decided to take a pause from my work and begin a Fibonacci sequence. *No sleeping bags...* 1, 1, 2, 3, 5, 8, 13, 21... I was beginning to feel better... 34, 55, 89, 144, 233, 377... I stared at the last number and took a deep breath. Then I reviewed my list and began packing again.

"Sunscreen."

That was all she wrote. She did not say what kind, or how many. *She seems very busy. I'll ask Jared.*

Jared did not live at our house. He lived in Egg Harbor, New Jersey. He worked for Atlantic Yachts, Incorporated. He was an engineer. He was spending the night at our house so we could leave at 5:07 in the morning. When I stepped into Jared's old room, I nearly killed myself on his luggage. (I exaggerated. I tripped.) Jared had piled everything in the middle of the floor. He was a slob. (That is not an exaggeration.) That was why we did not share a room when he lived at our house. That was before he went to college and before he married Erin Leigh McCann. Jared was a slob.

"Slob."

Erin Leigh McCann had to move out of Jared's house. She had sex with another man. My mother called it adultery.

"A-dul-t'ry."

Mom told me not to fixate on it. My therapist said I could ask Jared how he was doing, but I should refrain from calling his ex-wife a whore.

"Erin Leigh McCann the Whore."

Erin Leigh McCann was stupid.

Dr. Benjamin Conner Rush probably wouldn't like that, either.

I put my list in front of Jared so he could see it clearly.

"Sunscreen." I pointed to the word in Mom's handwriting. "How many bottles of sunscreen?"

"One. When she doesn't put a number in front of it, she means one. Pack one bottle of 30 SPF."

Jared got it right that time.

CHAPTER THREE

MATHIEU

Angelica was determined to go, and it ripped my heart out. Adding insult to injury, she implied that I was one of the reasons she felt so inclined to get away. I was completely devastated, but I could not let her see that. I took a deep breath, gave it considerable thought, and decided that keeping her on a tight leash would only validate her sentiments.

"Is Camille going with you?"

"No. She doesn't know, yet."

"Then who's going with you?" Her plans were beginning to concern me.

"No one. This is my trip. This is for me. I don't want any interference."

I took a deeper breath; my head began pounding with the stress I was working so hard to conceal.

"I get it," I resigned.

"Sadly, I think you do."

I took her into my arms. Angelica and I were the products of two very controlling families. I was beginning to recognize similar traits in the ways I responded to her. I wanted to give her everything. I craved her adoration and dependence. I had to find a way to back off while giving her all that I desired to lavish on her. I was beginning to recognize that my need for her dependence on me was the very thing that was making her run. I had to let her go. The fact that my ring was on her finger gave me hope that she would be the butterfly that always flew home.

I would miss her terribly. I could not imagine how I was going to fill my time while she was away. During a normal week, I would pick her up after work, and we would go out for dinner. Occasionally, we would go back to her place to share dinner with her roommate, Camille. Weekends belonged to me, and I always tried to have something special planned for her. We had visited many of the art museums and attended several concerts at the various venues in and around Philadelphia and New York City. One weekend we took a quick trip to Kiawah Island, South Carolina, to play golf. One of her favorites was a ten-day vacation we enjoyed in Hawaii.

When Angelica wasn't with me, I saw her in everything I did. I would call her on a whim just to hear her voice. Toward the end of every workday, I would become fidgety knowing that I would see her soon. The days that required me to put in extra hours almost sent me over the edge. At the end of those days, I would race over to her place to see her, if only for one kiss. Ironically, I had become dependent on her. Angelica's passion was like a drug, and I was the addict. I could not wait for the time when she would be completely and utterly mine.

The nights she did not think she should stay over, I would beg her to change her mind. "Stay the night, Angel. I'll make sure you get home by early morning," I would cajole. Several times I had suggested that she keep extra clothes and anything else she needed at my place.

I would miss her company and friendship during her time away. I would especially miss her in my bed at night.

JARED

Jarvis would get "stuck" sometimes. I got that, but not everyone else did. If you didn't understand him, he could wear you out. Over the years, I had learned a few tricks to help him "reset," and he had a good tool set of his own. Jarvis loved astronomy. Ask him anything about the stars and planets, and he would soon forget whatever it was that was bugging him and begin expounding on the constellations and things of the universe. While away, we planned on doing some stargazing whenever the skies cooperated. He was very excited about that part of our trip. He had read about the clear expanse of skies out west away from the East Coast's cities' glare.

The other things that helped him cope in uncomfortable situations were numbers and dates. He loved numerical sequences, calendars, and statistics. Ask him anything about an NFL game that he had watched or read about, and he could give you a play-by-play commentary. Be prepared though, in his mind he was never wrong. The way he saw it was the way it went down. Period.

I played football in high school, and Jarvis was my number one fan. He attended every game. Afterward, I would take him to an ice cream parlor, The Brown Cow, and he would give me a rundown of my best and worst plays of the game. Keep in mind; he was only in 1st, 2nd, or 3rd grade at the time.

Once I tried taking Jarvis out with the team to celebrate a "come-from-behind" win. I thought he would enjoy hanging out with the big guys. It was a total disaster. Our quarterback, Brett Short, recalled a play very differently than Jarvis did; one that Jarvis just had to bring up over and over again at our postgame celebration. Jarvis was hung up on the interception thrown early in the first quarter. I was the intended receiver. However, Brett overthrew the football and Downingtown's infamous cornerback easily pulled it in. Touchdown. As the argument ensued, Brett became increasingly agitated with my first grade brother. Jarvis, frustrated by Brett's refusal to admit his mistake, called Brett a "stupid ass." It was the first time I had ever heard Jarvis swear. My laughter did not help the combative atmosphere.

My buddies and I had to stand between Jarvis and Brett. What a sorry sight to see a little six year old get under the skin of a high school senior quarterback. Needless to say, I made sure their paths never crossed again.

Jarvis's mind was a steel trap. He could remember the smallest details, and rarely was his recall flawed. His world was spelled out in black and white, or explained by simple and complex equations. Making conjecture and supposition was completely meaningless to Jarvis. Because he innately lacked empathy, *or so I thought,* using any form of tact was a waste of time, too. His acute memory and social deficiencies often acted as an accelerant and ignited his sudden outbursts. Jarvis was understandably oblivious to the results, so Mom and I were the ones left to pick up the pieces.

My mom was a saint. She constantly reminded me that who we were as a family had the potential to withstand any judgment levied against us by an individual or institution. She believed that if we capitalized on our individual strengths, then our family team had the power to overcome whatever hurdles social norms placed in our lane during the so-called "race of life." She firmly believed that *"suffering produced perseverance; perseverance, character; and character, hope. And that hope would not put us to shame."* (Exploiting it for her personal agenda, Mom loved to paraphrase the Bible.) Regardless, she contended that my younger brother was happy in "the world according to Jarvis."

Outside the walls of our home and the security of our family, our mother had a fierce protective streak. I was keenly aware that she worried about Jarvis more than she let on. Our father left us when Jar was in the third grade, and his issues had become increasingly disruptive. (I called him "Jar" on occasion. One-syllable names are just easier sometimes. He never called me anything less than Jared.) My dad couldn't handle my mom's constant advocacy on my brother's behalf. Whether she was on the phone with his teachers, making appointments with therapists, reading articles on autism, or having a good cry, my dad was tired of hearing about it. He yelled at Jarvis, a lot. He didn't have the patience for Jarvis's obsessions. One day when I returned home from school, Mom was crying and Dad was gone.

I clung to Jarvis in those days. Not physically, he would never allow that, but I kept him in my sight. I feared that Mom might send him away if he caused any more trouble. She was a little crazier than usual then. Our house was upside-down, and I just didn't know what to expect. Shortly after Dad's departure, Grandmom Mathers came and stayed with us for a month, maybe longer. (Jarvis could probably tell you exactly how many days.) Grandmom Mathers assured me that Mom would never send Jarvis away. I do not know what I was thinking. I guess I was a little crazy then, too.

Jarvis, on the other hand, kept up his usual antics. He was probably the only predictable force in our household at the time. We could always count on Jarvis to pitch a fit if things were not to his liking. His behavior seemed to be the only remnant of stability in our lives.

Leaving for college a year later proved to be difficult. I was miles away from my brilliant buddy and biggest fan. I worried a lot about my mother and little brother in those days.

A decade later, packing for our trip out west was proceeding relatively well, thank God.

MATHIEU

I could understand Angelica's need to find a place where she could think things through without distraction or interference. What I struggled with was why so far away? And, more than that, I was very concerned with her determination to travel alone. She claimed that she would be fine, but I found it hard to believe that a woman as beautiful as she would ever be completely safe on her own.

I knew if I pressured her to stay or to take a companion, she would run harder and faster. Angelica was not like any other woman I had ever dated. She had a fierce independent streak that was tempered only by her parents' equally strong guardianship. From what I could tell, her trip would surely be the beginning of her break from their tethers.

Was she concerned that I would replace their harnesses with several of my own?

CHAPTER FOUR

JARED

Jarvis and I arrived at the airport on time, and things were running smoothly. Approaching the security check, I prayed that the TSA agents would not find a reason to search my brother. I did not want the trip to begin with a scene and then have to fly for the next five hours with the same on-lookers.

Fortunately, we passed through security without a hitch. Not everyone was so lucky. I looked over and saw a young lady being detained. I watched closely with a suspicious eye. One wrong move and I would … well actually, I don't know what I would have done. She was obviously uncomfortable with the proceedings. Anyway, I watched as the TSA agent patted her down and eventually allowed her to move on. She looked frazzled as she gathered her things and made sure her carry-on was closed and latched securely. It appeared she was traveling alone.

Jarvis snorted, signaling his impatience.

The incident was over, and we were on our way to Las Vegas. The young lady who was patted down was on our flight and seated in first class. I knew this because when we boarded the plane, she was escorted left, and we turned right.

JARVIS

As soon as we reached our cruising altitude of 33,000 feet, the pilot announced that we were free to move about the cabin and that our flight attendants would be

around to serve refreshments and snacks. Beer cost
$6.00 and wine or mixed drinks cost $7.00.

      I do not drink alcohol. I tried 2 times with
disastrous results. The 1st time was on April 24, 2004. It
was 4 days after my 16th birthday. It was a Saturday night,
and my friends – who turned out not to be my friends –
invited me to their field party. I do not remember much
about the party, which was perplexing, because I always
remembered everything. Apparently, my "not-friends"
drove me home and left me on my mother's front porch.
My mother was hopping mad. (My mother liked the word
"hopping" to describe her anger. So, I will use it here.)
      "Hop-ping."
      The next afternoon, Mom lectured me about
discerning "who is and who is not" a good friend. I decided
then that I would never have any good friends, except Jared.
      The 2nd time I drank alcohol was on April 20, 2009.
It was a Monday night. It was my 21st birthday. It was also
the day Jared's divorce from Erin Leigh McCann the Whore
became final. My brother Jared, who was my only good
friend, took me to one of his favorite places. He said it was
a day worth celebrating. Jared ordered a frozen strawberry
daiquiri for me. It tasted very good. I really liked it. I had 1
drink. Jared ordered a Long Island Iced Tea. Jared had a
2nd, and a 3rd drink. Jared was stupid when he married Erin
Leigh McCann the Whore. Jared was smart when he got
divorced from Erin Leigh McCann the Whore. Then we
celebrated, and he got stupid again.
      "Stu-pid."
      Jared was funny when he got stupid the 2nd time.
      I drove Jared home to our house at 1:53 AM, on April
21st, 2009, the morning after my 21st birthday and the day
after he got divorced from Erin Leigh McCann the Whore. I
knew not to leave him on our front porch. Although, I
would have enjoyed watching Mom get hopping mad all
over again.
      "Hop. Ping. Mad!"

My therapist said I should refrain from alcohol at all times. My medication does not permit me to consume it. I did not tell Jared about that minor detail on my birthday, the day he got divorced from Erin Leigh McCann the Whore. If he needed to know, his name would have been on the pamphlets that came with my medications. However, Jared's name was not on the pamphlets, so Jared did not need to know.

When the flight attendant came alongside us with her big silver cart, Jared ordered 2 coffees: 1 for him and 1 for me. The coffees were free. Mom does not allow me to drink 1 cup of coffee, let alone 2 cups of coffee in the same morning.
"What she doesn't know won't hurt her," were Jared's exact words. He was wrong about that. It always hurts her. Jared can be wrong about many things.
"Gentlemen, your coffee. Cream or sugar?"
"Two creams and four sugars for him. Straight up for me, please." Jared knew me well. He got my order right.

JARED

We landed in Las Vegas, rented a car, and headed for the South Rim of the Grand Canyon. Jarvis was having a good day. We escaped Philadelphia Airport without incident. On the plane, he busied himself with puzzles, numerical sequences, and napped restlessly for the final two hours of our flight. While he rested, or at least pretended to, I chatted with the lady across the aisle from me. She was travelling to Las Vegas for a convention. She was one of the keynote speakers. She showed me pictures of her two children, ages 7 and 5. As she gazed at their photos, I could tell she was already missing them. A tear escaped and quickly rolled down her cheek before she could catch it. We exchanged business cards. I wished her luck with her speech. She wished us a great vacation and stated, "While the Grand Canyon is spectacular, Zion Canyon should not be missed." She continued with her endorsement of the canyon by emphatically advising, "Be sure to hike The Narrows."

~

Jarvis liked our rental car, a Chrysler 300. It was loaded with extras including a sunroof that Jarvis wanted open at all times, except when it rained, which was never. That was how we spent our drive time - sunroof open and the AC on high. It felt decadent, but it was vacation. We sped along US Rt. 93 south at 75-80 miles an hour. I had never seen so much parched dry land in all my life. The trip from Las Vegas to the Bright Angel Lodge on the South Rim of the Grand Canyon took a little over 4 hours.

During the drive we played "20 Questions" and "Ghost" until I got tired of losing. Then I introduced Jarvis to a game called "Two Truths and One Lie." I tried to make it personal in hopes of learning some new things about him that I may have missed while away at college and then subsequently stuck in my failed marriage.

"OK Jarvis, I'll go first. Tell me which of these three statements is a lie about me. One, I've never received a speeding ticket. Two, I've never received a parking ticket. And three, I've never been in a car accident."

"That is easy. You received a speeding ticket on December 31st, 2006, at 9:03 PM when you and Erin Leigh McCann the Whore were going to a New Year's Eve party. Mom said it was a good thing you got pulled over on your way *to* the party. The police did not stop you on the way home, and that was a very good thing."

"Her name is Erin Leigh McCann Lawson. Why is it that you can never say her married name?"

"It was only a matter of time: 2,634 days to be exact. My last name is Lawson. Hers is not."

"Legally, her last name *is* Lawson. The law still recognizes her as Mrs. Erin Leigh McCann Lawson."

"Then I shall call her Mrs. Erin Leigh McCann Looser-son. How is that?" He laughed at his own joke. Jarvis was on a roll.

"Whatever, Jar."

I didn't want to get into it with him. He never liked Erin. Standing beside me as my best man on our wedding day, Jarvis whispered it would never last more than 2,557 days. He made his prediction the exact moment I got my first glimpse of my beautiful bride on the arm of her father. It has been said that while everyone strains to see the bride, the real photo opportunity comes when the groom first sees his beloved.

At our wedding, that moment was no exception, and one of the two photographers caught it all. Erin and her father stepped into the opened doubled doors just as Jarvis leaned over and made his confident prediction.

"I give it no more than 2,557 days," Jarvis whispered in my ear.

Perhaps it was the stress of standing in front of 250 people. Perhaps it was the relief that Erin had actually showed up. Whatever it was, I found Jarvis's whispered prediction hilariously funny and snorted loudly. Trying to conceal my enormous faux pas, I raised my hand to my face and turned away from our guests. I completely lost sight of Erin as she made her grand entrance, "the most important moment of her life." The entire congregation of witnesses turned their eyes back on me to see what all of the commotion was about. Jarvis and I had managed to steal the spotlight from Erin's lifetime fantasy walk down the aisle.

I was reminded of how my brother and I had ruined her wedding day for the remainder of our married lives, all 2,634 days of it. It was all down hill from there. Jarvis's prediction was pretty damn close.

"OK, it's your turn, two truths and a lie about you."

"Jared?"

"What?"

"Do you still love her?"

"I don't know how I feel about her anymore. Play the game."

"OK."

We drove another mile before Jarvis came up with his two truths and one lie.

"One, I am 5 feet, 8 and ¾ inches tall. Two, I weigh 183.6 pounds. And three, Erin Leigh McCann Looser-son can eat my shorts!"

Jarvis barely got through the third statement before he began to laugh and snort. His hands were at his mouth, and his knees were drawn up to his chest as he rocked in the passenger seat and laughed himself silly. I pulled the Chrysler 300 off to the side of the road, unbuckled my seatbelt, got out of the car, and slammed the door shut behind me. That was a big mistake. I had intended to run around to his side of the car and pull him out. But Jarvis was quick. He pushed the automatic lock. "Click!"

"Open this door!" I pounded on his window.

Jarvis started laughing like a little girl. He did that whenever he got overly excited.

"No!" he eked out when he finally took a breath.

"Jarvis, open this door, or so help me..."

"No!" He was still laughing and enjoying the amount of control he was exercising over me as well as the situation he had created.

I pulled my iPhone out of my back pocket.

"Jar, open this door or I'm calling Mom and you will have to go home." I pressed the screen of my cell phone up against the window so he could see Mom's picture and cell number up and ready for me to touch "Call."

Jarvis stopped laughing.

"You would not do that."

"Oh. Yes. I. Would. One, it's 100 degrees out here. Two, I am not laughing. And three, I love standing out here while the motor is running, and you are in the AC." A tractor-trailer flew by and blasted its horn making me jump.

"Jarvis!"

"OK, OK. I got this. The first statement is a lie because it's 103 degrees out there, to be exact."

Jarvis was completely serious. He stared ahead straight-faced.

"JARVIS! It's 103 degrees out here. I am not laughing because this is not fun for me. And, do you see this cell phone? I am going to call Mom."

"That is not how you play the game. None of those statements are lies! They are truths. Actually, the third is a threat, so it does not count. Play it right. Try again." He sat back in his seat and folded his arms across his chest.

"Dammit all!"

As a rule, I tried not to curse in front of Jarvis, but I was irate. It was extremely hot. There was not a breath of air, and the heat from the motor was making me hotter still. The fact that he could keep it up was pushing me over the edge.

"All right then. One, I'm going back to my side of the car. Two, You are going to unlock the doors. And three, I am going to get in and kill you. Which statement is a fucking lie, Jarvis?"

"All 3 are propositions, and the third remains a threat." He was unflappable.

"JARVIS!"

"OK. You can come in."

"Click!" The doors unlocked.

~

We arrived at the Bright Angel Lodge on the South Rim at 6:30 PM. Our bodies were sore and tired, but as you can imagine, the first thing we had to do was walk to the rim to see what all of the fuss was about. For me, it was a spiritual experience. In that moment, I knew there had to be a God. The enormity of it all was more than I could take in, and I was completely overwhelmed. It could have been the altitude, or it could have been the depth of the canyon painted with a palette of earth tones hung across an infinite horizon that blew me away. Stretched out before us, it all

served in making me woozy. Perhaps it was the wind
that whipped around with its hot dry air sometimes laced
with a layer of cold rush dropped from the sky. It created a
dizzying mixture. I had to re-center myself: two feet on
solid ground, flexed knees, and breathe deep.
Contemplating the magnitude of force and time that must
have been at work to create such a gargantuan
phenomenon, I stood silently balanced between the past
and the present. It was way beyond the limits of my
comprehension and far surpassed my scope of imagination.
    Jarvis seemed unfazed. He began reciting the
Canyon's dimensions followed by a disquisition of
geological theories. Given that emotion was virtually
missing from his assembly, *or so I thought,* I would have
said that Jarvis was duly impressed.

    The Bright Angel Lodge, like every other man-made
thing on the South Rim, had an authentic feel. It was rustic
and fashioned in early Native American. While I checked in
and patiently waited to receive the keys to our cabin, I
could feel Jarvis fidgeting next to me. With consideration
given to the time change, we were well beyond his expected
dinnertime. Quite frankly, I was in need of a beer from the
moment Jarvis had locked me out of the Chrysler 300. After
receiving our keys, we left the luggage in the car and
walked straight to the restaurant. After an hour wait, we
were seated at a table with a magnificent view of the
Canyon. As the sun, which paled in size to the Canyon,
began to drop from the sky, the Canyon seemed to change
as its colors took on an orangey hue, and its shadows
became longer and deeper. It created the illusion that the
Canyon was actually changing in dimension. I wondered
what a sunrise to sunset time-lapsed video would look like.
I was sure it had been done. I would search for it on
YouTube once we returned to civilization.
    It had been a long day, and I ordered that beer.
Jarvis asked for a club soda.
    "How can you drink that stuff?" I asked him with a
sour look.

"How can you drink that stuff?" He fired back.

"Because I can." I was exhausted and irritable. It probably was not the appropriate thing to say to someone who had to abstain. I certainly would not have said anything like that to a reformed alcoholic. I was just feeling dirty and mean.

It was dawning on me that sharing a room with Jarvis for the next two weeks was going to be draining. I was not going to get a break. Our trip had the potential to result in just the opposite of what it was intended to be. It was supposed to be about quality Jarvis and Jared time. I had high hopes that our trip would help Jarvis gain some self-sufficiency and a taste of independence he could not experience at home. Our mother had her doubts about my intentions and was reluctant to send Jarvis with me. I was beginning to have my doubts, too.

As soon as I opened the door to our cabin, all hell broke loose.

"It is all wrong. It is facing the wrong way!" Jarvis began throwing a fit. His hands were on his head above his ears and tugging at his hair.

"I face north! My head always faces north!" he pointed forcefully.

I quickly shut the door and tried to keep the one-man-meltdown from spilling out into the other nearby cabins.

"OK, OK, we'll turn the beds," I said to calm him down.

I grabbed ahold of the footboard of the bed farthest from the door and turned it so Jarvis's head would be facing north. That also meant I had to shift every other piece of furniture in the cabin to make it all fit again. I knew I had to accomplish some sense of symmetry and division, or Jarvis would not fully recover, and then we would have to start all over again. Hopefully, a correctly reassembled room would enable him to reset.

Not wanting to draw attention to the goings-on of Cabin #107, I rearranged the furniture as quietly as I could.

I was unsuccessful. It was not long before I heard a tapping on the door. Jarvis got to it before I could.

"Is everything OK?" a sweet voice quietly asked.

"No, it is not!" Jarvis scolded as if the unsuspecting soul was somehow directly responsible.

"It will be," I broke in. "I just have to do a little rearranging so my brother's head is facing north." How does one explain the reconstruction of cabin #107 in one complete, rational, and cognitive sentence?

"Oh, want some help?" Her dimples indented a little deeper as she smiled. It made me feel flush. I am always a little nervous around beautiful women. I was sure she could tell. Experience also told me that an unknown, albeit beautiful, woman in our cabin would throw Jarvis into further distress, so I had to decline her offer.

She seemed to understand and wished us a good night. Strangely, she resembled the poor victim held in security at Philadelphia International Airport.

MATHIEU

She had just arrived at the Grand Canyon and was standing on the South Rim when she called. How my heart swelled to hear her voice. She sounded so happy and rejuvenated. I held the phone out from my ear as she carried on about how magnificent her view was. She finally said the words I had been waiting to hear.

"Oh Mathieu, I wish you could see this!"

Well, close enough.

"I can be there in less than 7 hours!"

"Uh, no. Don't do that. That's not what I meant."

I would have dropped everything to rush to where she was. I had missed her terribly in just the few hours that she had been gone. That morning, I had hoped that she would change her mind before boarding the plane.

You see, very early and in a restless state, I sped to the airport and found her car in Parking Garage B. I looked at my watch. Her flight was due to take off in five minutes. I waited twenty. She did not return to her car, and her flight had indeed departed for Las Vegas. I was tempted to leave a note on her windshield, but I feared that upon her return my chase would send her running, again.

Angelica told me of her plans to hike down the Bright Angel Trail the next day. Knowing the dangers of that trail, I begged her to take a guide with her. I even volunteered to make the call for her. That only served to anger her.

"See, Mathieu, that's exactly what I'm talking about. I appreciate your worrying about me, but stepping in and trying to take control of my trip is not helping me. I don't want you trying to rearrange and fix everything for me all of the time. I am twenty-six years old, and I can take care of myself."

"Taking off and marching down the Grand Canyon is not taking care of yourself. People have died on that trail. Good people. Marathon runners. I don't want you hiking down there on your own." Unfortunately, I was fighting a losing battle, and she knew it.

"Mathieu, who says I'm hiking alone?"

JARVIS

The Grand Canyon is one of the 7 natural wonders of the world. It is 277 miles long. It is 7,000 feet deep at the South Rim and 8,000 feet deep at the North Rim. It is 18 miles across at its widest point. It covers 1,900 square miles or 1,218,376 acres.

The Grand Canyon was formed by erosion from the Colorado River, leaving layers of rock exposed. The bottom layer is 500,000,000 to 1,000,000,000 years old.

The Havasupai Native Americans needed access to water, so they built the Bright Angel Trail.

"Ha-va-su-pai."

In 1903, President Theodore Roosevelt Junior ordered the Havasupai tribe to leave in order to make way for the park. The National Park Service forced out the last of the Havasupai in 1928.

Did you know that President Theodore Roosevelt Junior did not have a middle name?

On June 6, 2010, at 6:05 AM, we started our hike down the Bright Angel Trail. The sign at the trailhead said that we had to stay on the trail. *Where did they think we were going to go?* The trail was only 3 feet wide in some places.

A stalker was following my brother.

"Stal-ker."

Her name was Angelica Orabelle Havens. She showed up at our cabin door the day before.

"Angelica who?" I asked through the cracked door.

"Use your manners," Jared scolded me. He had that look in his eye, the one that indicates when I have overstepped. I know Jared's signals. I am never wrong about Jared's signals.

"Angelica Havens," she answered.

"What is your middle name?"

"JARVIS!" Jared scolded me, again.

"What?" I shot back.

Like my mom, she did not hear me the first time.

"What is your middle name?" I asked a little louder.

Jared was not happy.

"Orabelle," she whispered.

I laughed. "Orabelle? Did you say Or-a-belle?"

We were hiking the Bright Angel Trail with Angelica Orabelle Havens. I thought her name was funny. Jared thought she was nice. Jared can be wrong about many things.

We had to wear backpacks and boots when we hiked. My backpack had a bladder in it. I laughed at that, too.

"Blad-der!"

I liked using that word.

The bladder was filled with spring water, not urine like most bladders. I laughed again. Jared frowned. Angelica Orabelle Havens snickered.

Maybe she is OK as far as stalkers go.

I did not laugh about my boots. They hurt my feet. Mom said I had to wear them on the trails. Mom made me practice wearing them at home. Jared practiced with me. We tossed the football back and forth while wearing our boots. I told Jared he looked like a dork. Jared said I was a dork.

"Dork."

We started our hike at 6:05 AM and ended at 2:47 PM. We hiked for 8 hours and 42 minutes. We covered 9.6 miles, making it to Indian Garden where we refilled our bladders.

"Ha ha! Bladders!"

Jared told me to start calling it a camelback.

I saw 8 lizards and 9 cliff squirrels. We did not see any snakes. Angelica Orabelle Havens was glad we did not see any snakes.

Jared and I used special hiking poles. They extended just like the ones that the park rangers used. When we started hiking back up the Canyon, Jared gave his hiking pole to Angelica Orabelle Havens. I said she could not hike back with us unless I knew the meaning of her middle name. She said it meant "Beautiful Seacoast." She was definitely in the wrong place. I think Jared likes Angelica Orabelle Havens the Displaced.

"Jared likes Angelica Orabelle Havens the Displaced."

Jared told me to shut up. He pulled me back and told me I was wrong. I am never wrong.

"Jared does not always lie. Sometimes, Jared might choose to avoid the truth." That was what my therapist, Dr.

Benjamin Conner Rush, said. According to Dr. Benjamin Conner Rush, Jared avoids the truth, and my mother speaks untruths. He said they do that to protect me.

Angelica Orabelle Havens the Definitely Engaged had a big diamond ring on her left ring finger. That was the truth. Jared was either blind, or avoiding the truth.

JARED

The second day of our trip we hiked down the Bright Angel Trail on the South Rim of the Grand Canyon. We started early in the morning to beat the afternoon heat. Smart move.

At first, I was nervous about having Angelica tag along with us. However, she was kind and patient with Jarvis. I rationalized that female company was one more thing Jarvis needed to get used to. Plus, she looked fit enough to handle the rigors of the climb.

I was married once before, and the truth was Jarvis never accepted my ex-wife as his sister-in-law. He never accepted her, period.

Jarvis would lower his head and whisper, *"Erin Leigh McCann Looserson the Whore."* Most often he would follow his mutters with a smirk. He did that a lot. He repeated words, names, or phrases that he had just heard or prized. Mom said he was trying to see if he liked the way the name or word rolled off of his tongue or felt in his mouth. To him it was like tasting a new candy for the first time. Believe me, Erin's name never tasted like candy to Jarvis. Except revenge *is* sweet. So perhaps it was his way of having his "just desserts."

Jarvis completely lost it when I first told him our backpacks would have built-in bladders. I remember when he first tried on the word "bladder." I could tell he really liked it. It made him laugh. I think he repeated it no less than three times in two minutes. Of course, Jarvis could tell you exactly how many times he repeated it over exactly what period of time.

I stayed close to Jarvis when we were hiking the narrow trails. I was fearful of his reaction if a passer-by shoved or bumped into him. Long stretches of the trail were perched precariously high above the canyon floor, and I did not want Jarvis to lose control and cause a potentially hazardous situation. Fortunately, he was OK when we had to step aside to let the mules go by. I reminded him that we were going to ride the mules the next day.

"I know that," Jarvis scoffed.

Of course he did. He probably had our itinerary committed to memory right down to the second.

The hike down was pleasurable. The temperatures were in the low 60s, and the air was dry. We stopped periodically for pictures. One of my favorite photos was of the three of us posing with the Canyon as our backdrop. I was in the middle of Jarvis and Angelica. Jarvis would not allow me to put my arm around his shoulder, but he did lean in slightly when our volunteer photographer, who was using my cell phone, suggested that we do so. When Angelica leaned into my body, my arm went naturally around her shoulder. She was wearing the biggest smile, and I looked handsomely happy. Jarvis was looking at the ground. It was a picture I would come to cherish forever. I forwarded it home to our mother in an effort to provide proof that all was going well. Of course, she wanted to know, "Who is that beautiful girl standing so close to you in the picture?" I knew that would get her attention!

No matter how hard we tried to capture what God had laid out for us to ponder, our pictures of the scenic views and vistas were not adequate enough. However, that one photo of the three of us on the precipice of a large fall clearly defined us.

The hike back up was grueling. All three of us were in great physical shape, but the return trip to the rim taxed every muscle, especially our cardiac and pulmonary systems. Once the sun rose to its noontime height, the Canyon heated quickly, and we had no choice but to climb through it. We took breaks in what little shade we could find when it was provided by an overhanging rock or a sparse tree. I recalled a sign we saw before starting out in the morning. It cautioned:

> "Down is optional.
> Up is Mandatory."

There was no way out other than under our own strength and resolve.

Angelica was without a hiking pole, and she was wearing down under the physical stress and mental challenge of the steep retreat to the rim. Telling her that my hiking pole was not helping me all that much, I gave it to her. In the wake of my bold face lie, Jarvis's facial expression was priceless. He immediately separated himself from us and continued his steady pace. He was relentless on that climb. Angelica and I worked hard to keep up.

When we finally arrived back at the summit, we were all hot, sweaty, and exhausted, except for Jarvis. He looked like he had been out for a walk in the park.

Sitting on the bench outside our cabins, Angelica began to recover after fifteen to twenty minutes of rest. Her glossy brunette hair blew carelessly around her face. Her dimples came back to her smile as she laughed at the stories I shared about Jarvis and me growing up. Jarvis snorted and went inside.

"He'll be OK," I said when he was out of earshot.

"I know. I think he handled the trail better than we did," Angelica commented and waved her hand between the two of us. Her ring caught the sun and burned a hole in my retinas. (Jarvis would have said that I was exaggerating.) It reminded me that she was spoken for. I took it as a sign from above. *God, she's beautiful!*

As she stood to say good-bye, her outstretched arm handed back my hiking pole. I felt a twinge in my heart as I reached toward her and took the pole from her hand. My eyes caught hers. They were beautiful, but the moment was here and gone. It was like tracking a shooting star. It was a pleasant surprise that faded all too quickly. When her gaze burned out, I detected sadness in her soul that seemed all too familiar.

"Angelica, would you like to join us on our mule ride along the rim tomorrow?" The words were out of my mouth before I could swallow them back.

~

"This is our trip, Jared. Our trip. Remember?"

Back inside our cabin, Jarvis was not thrilled about spending another day with Angelica Orabelle Havens the Party Crasher. Jarvis had given Angelica a new name. I thought it was funny. Jarvis was not laughing.

"I'm sorry, Jarvis. What's done is done."

MATHIEU

She implied that she would not be hiking alone. That was good news. What troubled me was the way she said it. Her voice inflection was exacted to tease, and it worked.

Angelica was completely unaware of her beauty. No matter how many times I told her, she always blushed and shrank away from my poetic compliments. She was vivacious and made everyone around her, especially me, feel alive. On the links she was a fierce competitor. Her upper body strength and focus gave her the ability to drive a ball as well as any pro. She did not take herself too seriously, and that allowed her companions to have a good time while she beat their pants off.

That was exactly what she would do to me. After a morning of 18 holes or an afternoon of doubles on the tennis court, I would impatiently wait to get her back to my place where we could play games at which she was also very good. Angelica knew how to relax and enjoy pleasure. Her unrivalled lovemaking never failed, and her timing was impeccable. She enjoyed taking me to the limit. Then, preventing me from boiling over, she would gently back off and sustain me at length on simmer. When she was good and ready, her teasing would drive me beyond the point of no return. She always managed to seize the upper hand, and she always maneuvered us to rise together.

My reminiscing only served to magnify my loneliness. Hopefully, my concern for her trip was overblown.

JARED

That night, in an effort to make peace, I took Jarvis stargazing. We found a clearing on the rim about an eighth of a mile from our cabin. I spread out a blanket, and we stretched out on our backs. It was a new moon, and the sky was crystal clear with no humidity to cloud the brilliance of the night's celestial display. Not many things impressed Jarvis. I thought his emotional deck was missing most of its cards. However, when he took his first look up, he gasped.

"Wow…"

Rarely does one ever hear that utterance from my brother. The only time I could remember hearing anything remotely close was when Jarvis was in the 3rd grade, and the Hale-Bopp comet passed by. It was 1997. (Jarvis could tell you the exact date, day of the week, and time.) The second time was when he viewed the Andromeda Galaxy through a high-powered telescope at the Franklin Institute in Philadelphia. That was how I knew Jarvis was truly impressed with the night sky above the Grand Canyon.

Jarvis aptly pointed out constellations that seemed to be hovering just above our heads. He said there were so many stars that he had to work a little harder to find the more familiar ones.

"Show off," I quipped.

That made him happy.

Before we knew it, it was well past Jarvis's self-regimented bedtime. I was surprised that he had not sounded the alarm. The carpet of glitter above us must have transfixed him.

"Cassiopeia is chained to her throne. See?"

"Where?" I asked.

"There." Jarvis pointed to the bright and beautiful heavens above us. "See the 'W?' That is her throne. It spins around the pole star and she spends half of her time upside down."

"Oh? Why is that?"

"She is being punished. Severely." He sounded as though he was the one responsible for levying her sentence."

"What did she do?"

"She was boastful, proclaiming the unsurpassed beauty of her daughter, Andromeda."

"Oh."

We lay quiet for a long time. A shooting star graced the sky, and I made a wish. Actually, I made two.

At some point, I had nodded off. The day's activity had taken a heavy toll on my body, and I was dead tired. To my knowledge, Jarvis stayed awake and focused on the sky. In my half-sleep, I could hear him mumble from time to time. The chill in the air settled into my joints and finally woke me up.

"Jarvis, do you know what time it is?" I asked, trying not to rile him.

"It is 11:47 PM," Jarvis answered very astutely.

"We need to get back. We have an early start in the morning."

Jarvis took one last look at the sky from his reclined position and whispered *"Andromeda,"* sighed, and said, "Okay."

When we reached our deck, I noticed Angelica was leaving hers. She quietly pulled her door shut behind her.

"Good evening! Where are you going?" I called out in a strained hush.

"Shhhhh! You'll wake my roommate!" She was terse and rushed off into the night. *I didn't know she had a roommate.*

"An-dro-me-da..." Jarvis whispered under his breath.

CHAPTER FIVE

ANGELICA

When the alarm rudely woke me, I rolled over and peered at the clock through one cloudy eye slit. Just as I had thought, it was much too early. Ugh! Up with the sun once again. Day three. After our hike down the Bright Angel Trail, I had accepted Jared's invitation to ride the mules along the rim. *What was I thinking?*

As the warm water poured over my aching body and sleepy eyes, my thoughts turned to Mathieu. He had taken my departure well. In light of my honesty, he had managed to not go postal on me. That was good. Perhaps he could relax, and we would be able to build our relationship on honesty and trust. But for some unexplained reason, I still had my doubts. My intuition kept telling me otherwise. Everything had been thrust upon me so fast that I was not allowed the time I needed to catch up with everyone else's plans for my life.

My parents loved me. I never doubted that. The three of us went everywhere and did everything together. My parents made room in their schedules for mother/daughter spa treatments and father/daughter golf and tennis outings. When I turned 16, I pleaded with my mother to tone down the birthday party she had planned for me. *Was the party for me, or was it all about her?* To some degree, she reluctantly complied. However, even after the event plans were pared back, the celebration was still a big bash that my friends talked about for weeks. They especially salivated over my birthday present - my first car, a 1995 Acura NSX-T.

"Daddy, is this car for you or for me?" I asked my father as we stood on the tarmac of our driveway surrounded by sixty-four of our closest friends and relatives. *Was it possible my father was living his second childhood through me?*

My bright yellow Acura, with its black detailing, was sitting pretty in our drive with its targa top removed. My dad threw me the keys and hopped into the passenger seat. Turning over the engine for the first time was exhilarating. Hugging the turns and accelerating in the passing lane, she handled like a dream. Once I was licensed, I was allowed to take her out on my own. After my first accident, my parents sold my Acura and bought a 1995 Ford Explorer. It was a tank.

Now ten years later, I felt like I was on a ride that was spinning out of control, and I could not locate the exit. Not that I wanted to. I just needed to know that I could open that basket door *if* I wanted to. I wondered, *"Which would be the riskier leap of faith: staying or going?"* I needed time and space to figure out if I really wanted the life Mathieu would possessively provide for us. It also struck me as odd how my parents seemed to be OK with the speed at which everything was moving. Only my dad took me aside the next evening and asked if I was OK.

"Quite the night, huh?" Dad asked as he sipped his martini.

"Yes, that it was. Don't you think this is all a little too soon? We've only been dating for 3 months?"

My father put his hand over mine.

"Angie, I knew in 3 minutes that I was going to marry your mother. In 3 weeks, I began making sure she would never look at another man. In 3 months, we started talking about our future."

"And when did you propose?"

"On our 6th month anniversary," Dad said beaming with pride. He clearly loved my mother as much as, if not more, than the day they first met.

"See, you had twice as long as I did to make sure you were right."

"True," my dad pondered. "If you're not sure, make it a long engagement. He seems like a very nice man. You'll want for nothing, that's for sure."

"What I want is what you and mom have."

"We had you, Angie. You were the answer to all of our dreams, and now we want you to be happy, safe, and secure for the rest of your life."

While we were having our manicures on the following day, my conversation with my mother was much different.

"So, have you thought about a wedding date?"

"No. I'm still trying to get used to being engaged."

My manicurist admired my ring and smiled. "You must be very happy," she assured me. "Surely a man who can afford a ring like that can afford to keep you very well, too!"

My mother was pleased. "Yes, he's a wonderful man. He is the sole heir of Dufour Winery and Distributors," my mother gushed and lifted her head with an air of vain dignity and self-satisfaction.

"Mom, don't you think this is all a little too soon?"

"Darling, when you know it's right, why delay the inevitable?"

"But that's just it, how can I be sure it's right?"

"Well, your father and I knew right away."

"Well, maybe I don't."

"Do you love him?"

"I think I do. I just wish I'd had more time. I wish that Mathieu and I had talked about it first. He popped the question in front of the whole world without ever hinting about it before."

"In a hot air balloon a thousand feet above the earth," my mother added, swirling her hand in the air.

"How romantic!" my manicurist chimed in.

"You will never want for anything and neither will your children. He is magnificently handsome like your father, and he seems like a wonderful young man. He adores you, Angelica. Everyone can see that. You two will make a good team." That completed my mother's list of prerequisites for my marital bliss.

Bliss. Now that is a notion. I do not believe a couple should build their lives with bliss as the end goal. It smacks of a fantasy world for wannabe trophy wives. Fairy tales end with "happily ever after." That is why they are called "tales." They are stories that someone made up and the world perpetuates to take the fear out of our future reality. Otherwise, without the distraction of fairy tales, we might all commit suicide. It is a prime example of "false hope."

"Angelica," my mother interrupted my thoughts, "the Dufours and the Havens have a lot in common. Both families have worked hard to build their family fortunes. You and Mathieu are only children. You will inherit it all one day. You and Mathieu are both savvy individuals and will do well together. Your children will be set for life. You'll have it all. And, God knows, the man is sexy as hell," my mother continued on the way home. She looked over at me with a mischievous glint in her eyes.

"MOTHER!"

"Oh, come on, Angelica. You're 26. We should be able to talk about sex. Sex, sex, sex. There. Get over it."

I did not want to talk about sex with my mother. She did not belong in Mathieu's bed, or mine for that matter. Her rhetoric left me feeling like I was being sacrificed for a kingdom.

I openly shared my fears with Mathieu. He chuckled at first, but he seemed to understand. His life had been carved out for him as well. It was understood that he would one day take sole possession and control of the Dufour empire.

After he held me at arms length and stared into my eyes for what seemed an eternity, he said, "OK. I get it."

That was it. He never mentioned it again. The night before my departure, he kissed me good-bye and lamented on how much he would miss me. I assured him that I would call when I arrived in Las Vegas and again when I reached the Grand Canyon. I could hear the disappointment in his voice and feel his concern through the muscles of his arms and the tightness of his chest as he swallowed me in his embrace.

"Mathieu, this is not about you. It's about me. I just need time away, to think things through."

I only wish I could have been as honest with my parents.

That was the other thing that was beginning to undermine my relationship with Mathieu. All of my life I had lived in the financially secure cocoon of my parents' bank accounts. I do not want to sound ungrateful, but I had no real sense of accomplishment until I secured my first job teaching 2nd grade in a small public elementary school. Marrying Mathieu so soon would send me from my parents' welfare to his. I was sure my parents were relieved to know that I would be well provided for under Mathieu's wide umbrella. However, umbrellas can get turned inside out very quickly. Then what? I needed an umbrella of my own, not one that always covered my head with someone else's hand attached to it. I also wanted to avoid raising my children in the same overprotected welfare state that I was in.

How would Mathieu feel about that, … if he wanted children?

CHAPTER SIX

ANGELICA

"Good morning. How are you guys doing?" I asked as I joined Jared and Jarvis at the shuttle stop. Jared's face lit up and Jarvis's fell. They looked like the comedy tragedy masks I had seen on many Broadway playbills. It was all too obvious that Jarvis was not thrilled to see me again.

"We're doing great," Jared answered.

"You were out very late last night," Jarvis accused loudly.

"Shush." Jared grabbed his arm. "That's none of your business." Jarvis immediately shook off his brother with a vengeance.

"I just needed some air," I followed with hope that Jarvis could find reason enough in my explanation.

"She's lying," Jarvis whispered to Jared as if I wasn't standing there.

"It's OK, Jarvis, she just needed to go outside and get some air. Now drop it," Jared snarled between his teeth.

"Liar."

Jarvis was calling me out. I was hurt and I could not see his eyes to evaluate just how upset he was. More often than not, eyes speak louder than words. But Jarvis always hid his from me. Yet, his words rang true.

Jared politely suggested that my so-called roommate could have joined us on the trail ride had he known. I somehow avoided an explanation. Jarvis's eyes remained hidden from me, but I could tell he wasn't buying it.

We boarded a small shuttle bus that took us to the stables. I sat alone in a seat behind the Lawson brothers. As we came around the bend, I could see the mules saddled and lined up waiting for us to mount. As soon as I jumped down from the last shuttle step, someone asked me if I had ever ridden before.

I had ridden many times before. In fact, we owned several horses. I had taken riding lessons when I was in elementary school from a private instructor who boarded her horse at our stables in exchange for my lessons. By the time I graduated high school, I had competed in more dressage events than I could count. My annual circuit included the historic and nationally acclaimed Devon Horse Show.

"Have you ridden before?" the guide repeated as if I did not hear her the first time.

"Yes, a little," I answered sheepishly. I had a feeling Jared was watching me closely. I could never tell with Jarvis.

The guide adjusted the stirrups and then I mounted the mule without assistance.

"She is lying." Jarvis didn't miss much, especially for a guy who did not seem to notice.

JARED

I was worried about Jarvis. He had been on pony rides when he was little, but never anything that big and certainly not without a lead line. When the guide asked Jarvis if he had ever been on a horse, he answered, "Yes."

That was it. No more questions. I wanted to jump down and explain his situation.

He doesn't handle change well.

He has a difficult time when things fall out of his perceived sequence or don't meet his expectations.

Don't touch him or try to throw him up there!

"Martin, bring this gentleman 'Moe'." The guide looked at me over her shoulder. "That's 'Mo,' as in 'Slow-mo'," she winked and smiled. She must have sensed my anxiety. I looked back at Angelica who had already mounted her mule.

"He'll be fine," Angelica mouthed as if she had read my mind.

The guide took her time getting Jarvis up and into the saddle of Mo. She never touched him. She showed him how to put his left foot up in the stirrup, pull his body weight up using the saddle horn, and throw his right leg over the saddle. She demonstrated as she talked him through it. Then she coached Jarvis, step-by-step, or should I say, stirrup-to-stirrup. He was up and ready. She instructed him to keep the reigns loose and his heels down.

Fortunately, Jarvis was strong enough to throw his own weight over the mule and into the saddle. Only he and Angelica managed it without one of the guides pushing their butts up and over - mine included.

Since Jarvis's first fight in middle school, I had worked out with him every chance I got. I had decided that if Jarvis was going to pick fights with everyone who disagreed with him, or touched him, he'd better know how to defend himself and have more muscle mass than the other guy. More importantly, I encouraged him to use his words first before resorting to his hands. The second instruction was not going as well as I had hoped. Much to my mother's despair, Jarvis had returned home from school several times sporting a split lip or a bloody nose. In each instance, Jarvis had instigated the rumble. Sometimes, I worried that I may have gone too far with his physical training, and that one day he might really hurt someone.

After everyone was on his or her mule, we started down the trail in a specific order that was dictated by our lead guide. She put Jarvis right behind her, after Jarvis was Angelica, and I followed Angelica. Four other people completed our group.

True to what we had been told, the mules clung to the outside of the trail. Jarvis was oblivious to the danger, Angelica rode like she had been doing it all her life, and I was a wreck. I tried to keep my eyes on Jarvis while making sure my mule did not misstep, run me into a low hanging branch, or sideswipe a tree trunk. I was sure the view was breathtaking, but honestly, I was too focused on the task of staying on my mule and that it stayed on the trail. Ahead of me, I could hear Angelica trying to make small talk with Jarvis, and I also noticed his thorough lack of acknowledgement. *It's a good thing Jarvis is not looking for an intimate relationship anytime soon.*

I recalled the numerous times I told Jarvis that one day he would like girls as much as I did. I remembered the first time he was upset because I chose to take my then girlfriend to the movies rather than stay home with Mom and him to watch TV. At the time, he was 8 years old and utterly repulsed by my choice.

A couple of times, Angelica swung around in her saddle to point out various things she was interested in. I had to ignore her last several observations, including a condor soaring below the rim on the canyon's updrafts. Looking out and over the long drop atop a moving mule was making me queasy. I said, "Oh, cool!" without really looking. I think she knew. Angelica seemed very perceptive, too.

~

That night at dinner, I noticed that Angelica was in the lodge restaurant eating alone. She must have gone early to dinner. By the time Jarvis and I arrived, we were greeted by a thirty to forty minute wait, so I decided to pay Angelica's table a visit.

"Hi! Where's your roommate?" I thought it was an innocuous question, but Angelica just blankly stared up at me. No Response. *Was she mad? Did I say something wrong?*

"Have a seat, Jared." Angelica motioned toward the empty chair next to her. "Please?"

I looked back at the hostess stand where Jarvis was seated on a bench and playing a game on his iPhone. I knew he would be fine if I left him alone for a few minutes.

I pulled out the chair and sat down next to Angelica. Her elbows were on the table as she wrung her hands above her empty plate. Her overstated diamond ring was now larger than life as the sun shining through the full-view window reflected upon its perfect cut.

She was either stalling or lost in her thoughts.

"You roommate?" I gently tried to bring her back to earth.

Angelica took a deep breath, squared her shoulders, and turned to me.

"There is no roommate, Jared. I'm on this trip alone."

"Alone? Why? Not that I mean to pry, but why alone?" I nodded toward the rock on her finger.

"That's exactly why."

"What? I don't get it."

"I needed space."

"Oh..."

"Everything was going great until he proposed."

"So he became a jerk after you accepted his proposal?" I cannot even tell you why I said that. I did not know her fiancé, and it was the first time she had said anything about being engaged. Though, one could not miss the repellant rock on her ring finger.

"Not exactly. He's always been a perfect gentleman." Angelica dropped her hands into her lap. Her head lowered, too. Her reflective moment did not need a comment from me, and silence seemed to be the best filler for the space between us.

Her waiter showed up carrying her dessert. It was a huge lump of chocolate cake with hot fudge flowing from its center. We both chuckled after he set it down in front of her.

"Drowning your sorrow in chocolate, I see." I tried to add a little levity to her sadness.

"Chocolate Lava Cake. Would you like to try some?" She dug her spoon into a side of the molten mass of warm comfort and held it up. "This stuff has super healing powers."

"Who said I ..."

She did not let me finish. As natural as natural could be, as if we had been friends all our lives, she lifted the spoon to my mouth and shoved it in. Her generosity left traces of sticky chocolate residue all around my lips. She got a good laugh out of that. Wow, it was good.

I did not know how long Jarvis had been standing there, but I suddenly felt his presence, and he was not laughing along with us as I licked the chocolate goo from the sides of my mouth.

"Hi, Jarvis!" Angelica lit up with a beautiful smile always accentuated by a deep dimple on either side. All of her heaviness disappeared instantly.

"Our table's ready." Jarvis said in a monotone drone indicating that he was annoyed.

"I'll be right there."

He turned away without acknowledging Angelica. I took a deep breath, and Angelica handed me her napkin to finish with the clean up.

"It's OK," she said, excusing my brother's slight. She must have noticed my frown.

"How long will you be here?" I asked, touched by her forgiveness and out of my genuine concern for her wellbeing.

"Oh, I'm going to go back to my cabin, pack up, and leave for the North Rim in the morning."

"Really?"

"That's the plan."

"How about that, so are we!"

Angelica and I agreed to meet up for breakfast in the morning, and then we would caravan up to the North Rim together.

"Oh, and Jared, my friends call me Angie."

When I took my seat at the table, Jarvis was still pre-occupied with his video game. I knew better than to interrupt him. I was keenly aware that Angelica, uh... Angie... was sitting just a few tables away and finishing her chocolate dessert, alone.

I wondered what her fiancé was like and why he had allowed her to travel solo? More than that, there was something about her that held my interest in a way I could not quite get my head around. I tried to consider other things, like the best route to the North Rim, but it did not take long for my thoughts to drift back to Angelica... uh, Angie.

Back at the cabin, Jarvis began repacking everything into his duffle bag. He was throwing and slamming things around. Something had his hackles up.

"Jarvis! What is it? You didn't talk to me all during dinner. Now, you're slamming your stuff around. What's up?"

I did not have to ask. I already knew the answer.

JARVIS

"In case you haven't noticed, she's married."

"Engaged."

"Same thing. This is our trip. She doesn't belong."

"This *is* our trip, you and me. She just happens to be following the same itinerary. In fact, she's headed for the North Rim tomorrow, and we're going to caravan out together."

"See, that's just what I'm talking about. She's stalking us. She doesn't belong. Where's her roommate, huh?"

"There is no roommate."

"She lied."

"She just wasn't ready to let strangers know the truth."

"So, she lied."

"Whatever, Jarvis. Yes, she lied."

Jared can be so blind, especially when it comes to women.

The drive to the North Rim took 5 hours and 36 minutes. The first 3 hours were across the dessert. It was hot and dry. There were no trees for shade. There were no lakes or streams, just dried up washes. There were no restaurants, or people, or houses. The Chrysler 300 had a good air conditioner, but it was so hot we had to close the sunroof and pull the shade over the glass. The heat waves blurred the horizon. It had not rained there in a very long time. I did not think we would ever see green grass again. Dust devils, translucent with the color of sand, spun across the parched landscape. We could have died out there, and no one would know. Angelica Orabelle Havens the Party Crasher was behind us in her rental car. She would know. So, we were not totally alone. If our car broke down, she could go for help in her sporty rental Acura.

"It's OK that Angelica Orabelle Havens the Party Crasher followed us today," I told Jared to make him happy. "She can go for help."

"What?"

We were driving toward the mountains when we made a large "U" over the Colorado River and began our climb. The road narrowed as we drove through a series of switchbacks.

"Switch-backs."

Switchbacks are really cool. They made the climb up the Bright Angel Trail much easier. I liked the way it sounded, too.

"Switch-backs."

We finally stopped for lunch at a place called "Jacob's Lake." It was 29.4 miles south of Fredonia, Arizona. I found it. They made the best BLTs and French fries. They were just the way I liked them.

JARED

Before leaving the South Rim, Angie and I exchanged cell phone numbers so we could stay in touch during our drive. A little over 4 hours into it, she called and said she was in need of a pit stop. I agreed and added that it was time to get lunch, too. We were 80 percent of the way to the North Rim when we stopped at Jacob's Lake.

As much as Jarvis protested having Angie along, he promptly went to work on finding the closest restaurant to our location when asked. That was how we landed at Jacob's Lake. Parking our vehicles next to each other, Angie stepped out of her rental car and thanked us for stopping. She anxiously stated that she was in need of the break about an hour earlier. Needless to say, she made a beeline for the restrooms.

"Are you going to buy her lunch?" Jarvis whispered across the urinals.

"Of course, that's what a gentleman does." I pulled my fly up while Jarvis was still going strong.

"Suc-ker!" He sneered. Finally, finishing his business, he zipped up, thoroughly washed his hands as Mom had always instructed, and checked his gig line three times in the mirror.

We waited for Angie in front of the hostess desk.

"She's going to slow us down. She's going to take all of your money and slow us down. We won't be able to finish the trip or get anything nice for Mom." I noticed the hostess watching us as Jarvis loudly registered his complaints. "You're a sucker, Jared. *Suc-ker!*"

Seeing Angie enter the restaurant, I gave Jarvis a knowing jab with my elbow. He shoved me off.

"Will that be 3?" the hostess asked cautiously.

"Not unless you want to give this guy a job," I replied pointing my thumb in Jarvis's direction.

"Jared!" Angie half-scolded me as she approached. "Be nice."

Note to self: Angie has good ears – and she's perceptive!

The hostess seated us in a corner off to one side. Jarvis moved his chair as far from Angie as he could. Then he rearranged his placemat, silverware, and water glass so everything was parallel and equal distance. That was another one of his obsessions.

One of the many things we came to appreciate while out west was that as soon as you sat down at a table, a waiter would not be far behind to fill your water glass, and the water was delicious. There was no chlorine aftertaste that could be detected in city water back east. Jarvis immediately lifted his filled glass and emptied half of it. He knew how to stay hydrated. He had taken Mom's last minute demands seriously.

Jarvis ordered the BLT. It kept him busy and satisfied while Angie and I chatted over our salads. Angie finally got around to telling us about her fiancé, Mathieu Dufour. I didn't know him personally, but I certainly knew the Dufour name. Everyone in the tri-state area of Pennsylvania, Maryland, and Delaware knew of the Dufour family fortune.

"How did you two meet?" I asked, curious as to how their exclusive social circle worked.

"Our fathers introduced us. They play golf together at Pine Valley and arranged for us to play in a foursome," she replied and Jarvis snorted. Jarvis snorts whenever he disapproves or suspects something is awry.

"Ignore him." I leaned over and whispered close to her lovely face.

"It's all right. I understand. Everything with our two families is way over the top. I think I'm learning that living with Mathieu will be no different. You know, cut from the same mold. I don't know whether he is trying to impress me or everyone else around us."

"I wouldn't think a Dufour felt the need to impress anyone."

"Exactly. But everything seems to be for show. No, everything is a show, an advertisement to be exact. It's like whenever we're together in public, it's all about the family empire. We have to put on airs for the benefit of the business and the family name."

"That's got to be hard and tiring. If you don't mind my asking, does he know how to relax? Is it different when you two are alone and out of the public eye?"

Jarvis snorted his disapproval, again.

"It's hard to say. We've only been dating for three months."

Jarvis sprayed his water across his plate, once more failing to conceal his annoyance, or was he humored? Sometimes, it was hard to tell with him.

"Jarvis!" I scolded. "Get it together. You're in a restaurant."

Angie stared at her salad and pretended not to notice my attempt at disciplining my younger adult brother. I took a deep breath and turned my attention back to her.

"That's not a long time, Angie. He must be madly in love with you, which I can certainly understand," I commented while keeping my eye on Jarvis.

She blushed and shrank back into her chair. Jarvis twitched and coughed. I could not help but think how even more attractive she was because she was so natural and down to earth while having to navigate the airs and expectations of her prodigious fiancé and both of their families.

"Sorry, I didn't mean to make you feel uncomfortable."

"It's alright. Thanks for listening. How about you? Do you have a girlfriend?"

Jarvis snorted again and turned away to whisper, *"This ought to be good."*

"No. No girlfriend in the picture."

"No wife, either," Jarvis threw in his two cents and laughed raucously toward the wall behind him.

Thank God, the waitress showed up and asked if we were having dessert. I looked to Angie.

"Nothing for me, thanks."

"Jarvis?" He was still trying to regain control. I did not wait for his answer.

"I think we're done here. I'll take the check." I was tired of Jarvis's antics.

I insisted on picking up the check despite Angie's protests.

Back in the Chrysler 300, Jarvis let me have it.

"She is loaded, Jared. Her father plays golf with Mr. Olivier Montique Dufour at Pine Valley. She is engaged to someone she has only known for 3 months. It is all about the money, Jared. Stay away from her. Plus, her fiancé may not be here, but he is probably having her followed and you are going to get knocked off."

"Knocked off."

"Shut up, Jarvis. You watch too much TV. No one's going to get knocked off."

"Yes you are. That is the way it works. The girls get knocked up and the guys get knocked off."

I could only shake my head, which I did not think he would notice because he never looks at me.

"OK, shoot yourself." Jarvis laughed.

I swear, sometimes he thinks he is the smartest person on earth.

JARVIS

Jared knows nothing about women. He was married to one for 7 years, 2 months, and 18 days, but he did not learn a thing. I will stop myself here because I want to say, "whore," but my mom does not like that word, and Dr. Benjamin Conner Rush said I should stop saying it. The last time I said it, Jared was going to throw me out of the Chrysler 300 rental car.

"Whore."

There, I whispered it one last time. So, Angelica Orabelle Havens is going to marry Mathieu Olivier Dufour for his money. (I needed to know his middle name, so I googled it.)

His name is Mathieu Olivier Dufour. Who spells their name M-A-T-H-I-E-U, anyway, huh? I think Mathieu Olivier Dufour the Opulent and Angelica Orabelle Havens the Klingon were meant for each other.

I looked out the window of the Chrysler 300. I was relieved to see conifers, green grass, and wild flowers growing alongside the road. We passed a moose crossing sign, but never slowed down for the nonexistent moose. I was tired of looking at rocks. The changing ecosystem was a welcomed sight. As the landscape turned green and the temperature dropped, I felt like I had been holding my breath for the last 4 days, 9 hours, and 34 minutes.

In the lobby of the lodge on the North Rim, Jared took care of our cabin keys. Jared and I shared a cabin, again. I am OK sharing a cabin with Jared. I am not OK with Angelica Orabelle Havens the Klingon occupying the cabin next door. She likes men with money, and she lies.

JARED

Once again, I had to go through the exercise of rearranging the furniture in our cabin. On the North Rim, the exercise was a little more taxing because the cabin was smaller. Adding to my misery, Jarvis was in the way. The chaos I was creating to get all of the furniture moved around was sending him into a tailspin. I could feel him winding up. I always could. Sometimes I believed I

possessed a sixth sense when it came to Jarvis. He
started panicking when I could not get the second bed
turned and had to move other furniture to the far side of
the cabin in front of the fireplace, sort of in a clump, piling
one chair on top of the other. He started pulling at his hair
and yelling, "No, no, not like that!" I handed him a pad of
paper and a pen.

"GO. OUT. SIDE!"

"No."

"If you get out of the way, I can get this done."

"No. Get it right."

I wish I could say that Jarvis gave me the evil eye,
but Jarvis did not make eye contact, ever. I have never had
the pleasure or opportunity to stare-down my little
brother. He just stands there and looks down. When he
was younger, it was part of what made him such an easy
target for ridicule. No matter how hard I tried, I hated that
I could not fix him. If I spoke to him sternly, I could
eventually hold his gaze, but only for a moment. I hated
that it was not natural for him to look at the person
speaking to him, or worse, threatening him. Also, I could
not grab him or try to wrestle him into submission because
he would scream like a girl. I could not punch him because
when he hit back he could do considerable damage. I had
personal experience with his retribution, and I was partly
responsible for his "take no prisoners" reaction to a
physical attack. Quite frankly, I did not touch him because
for the remainder of the trip I would bear the pain and
scars that I personally knew he could inflict. Plus, the
whole scene would scare off Angie; I was sure of it.

I did not know why I even cared what Angie thought
or if she hung around any longer. She was going to go
home soon, anyway.

Jarvis stomped around on the small wooden porch
for about a minute or two before I heard him settle down.
Good. I worked quickly to get everything in its place before
he decided to come back in. I turned the dead bolt on the

door insuring that I would have enough time alone to finish the task.

Everything is in its place, there is a clear division between the two sides of the room, and Jarvis's bed is facing north. Mission accomplished.

I looked outside. Jarvis was gone. *CRAP!*

I called Jarvis's cell phone. After waiting several seconds, I heard it ringing in his backpack that was tucked away in a corner. I grabbed my keys and pulled the door shut behind me. *Oh, this is bad.* We had not done any exploration since our arrival on the North Rim. I really did not know where to start. I decided to enlist Angie's help.

I knocked several times. No answer.

"Angie," I called into the face of her locked door. "Angie, are you in there? I need your help." I waited for her response, but I did not hear any movement or sound coming from inside. I called her cell phone. No answer, and I could not hear it ringing, either. *Great, she must be out.*

I was on my own.

The North Rim was less populated and less touristy than the South Rim. It was tree lined rather than paved with sidewalks, parking lots, and shuttle stations. I started jogging with hopes that I would find him out for a leisurely walk. Jarvis was stronger than I was in many ways, and he could motor faster when he wanted to. I feared that I had really pissed him off. If he took off running, he could be a mile or two ahead of me. I had covered about a quarter mile when I spied him seated on a bench, and he was not alone. Sitting on the far end was Angie.

It was a curious sight. They were not talking, just staring out across the canyon. I ran up to them.

"What are you doing out here, Jarvis? You scared the crap out of me. Next time, tell me where you're going."

"I wanted to, but you locked me out."

"Jared, what were you thinking?" Angie asked accusingly. She reminded me of my mother.

"What? I didn't lock him out."

"You did. You asked me to leave. So, I left. I decided to go for a walk. I wanted to tell you, but the door was locked. You told me never to interrupt a man if his door is locked. The door was locked. So, I didn't interrupt. I went for a walk instead."

I was dumbfounded. I had no idea how to respond to that. I had no idea what Angie thought Jarvis's comment said about me.

"You could have knocked."

"That would be interrupting."

ANGIE

The North Rim brought me great peace. With its tall pine trees and cool summer temperatures, it reminded me of Maine. In the early morning hours, I had to light the gas fireplace in my cabin to abate the frost on the windows and warm the tips of my ears and nose.

When we first arrived, Jared was a perfect gentleman and helped me check in. He insisted on hauling my luggage to my cabin. Once everything I brought was in the door, he swiftly left stating that he had to get Jarvis settled. My cabin shared a wall with theirs, and as I was placing a few of my products in the bathroom, I could hear the disturbance. I quickly finished and went next door to see if they needed my assistance.

"Jarvis, what are you doing out here?"

"Jared locked me out."

"He did? We just got here. What happened?"

"The room is a mess and Jared is a slob. He made me leave."

"Jarvis, would you like to take a walk with me and give Jared some time to clean up his mess?"

"Yes, Angelica Orabelle Havens *the Klingon*," Jarvis laughed. He had lowered his head and whispered something after my last name. If I did not know better, it sounded like he said "the Klingon." I had to admit, coming from him it was funny.

"Is that how you see me, Jarvis? As a Klingon?"

"Yes."

"Jarvis, has anyone ever told you that you might want to be a little more subtle?"

"Yes. Dr. Benjamin Conner Rush tells me that all the time."

It felt good. I was actually having a conversation with Jarvis!

"So, there are times when it might be wise to temper what you say or how you say it?"

"Are you telling me I should lie? I don't lie."

"Of course not. Let's walk."

Jarvis and I walked until we found an opening in the pines and a bench where we could sit and enjoy an unobstructed view of the Canyon. No words were exchanged. We just sat.

Though I was sure he would tell it differently, it did not take long for Jared to find us. Blocking our view and looking frazzled, he stooped over and tried to catch his breath.

"You need to move." Jarvis was not asking; he was demanding.

"What? I just moved an entire room of furniture for you!" Jared looked hurt.

"This might be one of those times, Jarvis," I interjected, hoping he would remember our earlier very brief conversation.

"OK. Jared, you locked me out, and now you are standing in my way."

"What?" Jared was incensed and an argument ensued.

I just put my head in my hands and listened to their banter. It quickly moved to Jared's rule about not being interrupted when behind locked doors. Jarvis was very matter-of-fact about it. I think Jared was embarrassed. From where I sat, it was rather comical. I had to join the fun.

"So, Jared, just why was the door locked? We just got here," I chided.

Jared put his hands on his hips and shifted his weight from one leg to the other and stared at me as if to say, "Really? You, too?" His eyes were full of wit and blazing with sexy sardonic humor. I could feel the mutual heated chemistry flowing between the two of us. I had to look away. Our gaze was moving into dangerous territory.

~

That night, I spoke with Mathieu. Back home it was 1:00 AM, Eastern Daylight Savings Time. Needless to say, I woke him up.

"Hi, Sleepy Head," I whispered into the receiver.

"Hey!" I heard him shift under the covers. "Where are you?"

"I am out under the stars on the North Rim of the Grand Canyon and missing you.

"I miss you, too, Babe. When are you coming home?"

"I don't know. I may stay out a little longer."

"What? Really? I mean, why?"

MATHIEU

I trusted Angelica. It was everyone else that I did not trust. Her news of traveling out west to get away from "everything" and "everyone" hit me hard. I did understand. I really did. I used to feel the same way. But that did not make it any easier for me to let her go, especially after we had just gotten engaged. Her "everyone" must have included me or else she would have invited me to go along. While she was planning her escape, I was dreaming about spending the rest of my life with her. I was crushed. I felt like I had made a mistake; I had rushed her. But what was done was done.

I knew I had to let her go. Restricting her would make her run farther, longer. We had only been dating for 3 months, but I had learned a lot about her in that time. She had a gentle spirit. It was one of the things that drew me to her. However, when caged, she would furtively, yet fiercely, fight her way out. I feared that one day I would come back and find her gone. The one thing I thought would ease my mind, an engagement, had actually been the very thing that made her flee.

She also had a competitive streak that only showed itself when necessary. But when it did, she was unstoppable until she gained the upper hand. When that happened, she would leave you to choke on her dust.

So, I had to let her go, and do so without a fight.

What concerned me most was that she insisted on going alone. Only her roommate, Camille, and I were privy to her plans. Angelica said her parents would have worried, and her mother would have threatened consequences if she went alone. So, she "neglected" to tell them.

However, there was one thing that only I, and the person that I had hired, knew; Angelica was being followed.

ANGIE

That night, Jared, Jarvis, and I went out at midnight to watch the stars and satellites. Jared grabbed two blankets from their cabin and Jarvis's flashlight, and then the three of us headed out.

"Where are we going?" I asked. I found it strangely exciting that I was out in the middle of nowhere and moving through the dark with two men that I hardly knew. I had my cell phone with me, but the signal was hit or miss. The thought that I was actually living on the edge, figuratively and literally, gave me a chilling thrill.

What if these guys are maniacs and they're leading me out here so they can push me over the edge of the Canyon

*and watch me fall to my death? What if they befriended
me so they could lead me miles away from civilization, rape
and murder me, then throw me over the edge? If that's the
case, hopefully they will kill me first, and then do what they
need to do.*

We continued walking in the dark. The trees
seemed taller and the night noises louder. Jarvis was in the
lead, pushing ahead as Jared and I followed.

"How much farther?" I asked Jared.

"We're going to Bright Angel Point where there are
no lights to pollute the night sky."

"Well, there definitely aren't any lights out here." I
shivered.

"Are you OK?" Jared asked.

"Who, me? I'm fine." I lied.

"You lied." Jarvis did not miss the opportunity to
point out my offense.

"Not really, Jarvis. I'm speaking words that will help
encourage me."

"Interesting concept," Jarvis said, but I knew he
wasn't buying it.

"I believe that what you speak into yourself, and
others, can really make a difference."

Jarvis grunted.

"For example, if my parents had spent my life telling
me that I was a bad child, I'd probably turn out to be one."

Jarvis grunted again.

"So, what *did* your parents tell you?" Jared was
curious as he followed my theory, and I followed him and
his brother into the dark of night.

"I don't know. I remember them telling me I was
smart, and that I was able to do anything I put my mind to."

"Those sounds like good things to say."

"What did your parents say, Jared?" I asked hoping it
would give me more insight into the men I was blindly
following.

*Was I nuts? Mathieu would kill me if he knew I was
out here with two other men. He would be furious. It was
probably a good thing I had called him earlier in the night.*

I recalled his low voice and the rustle of his bedcovers. My mind drifted to how Mathieu's chest would rise and fall as he breathed deep in sleep. He would shift his weight, settle in comfortably, and always readjust the arm he kept wrapped around me to make sure I was still next to him. Nestled in his warm strength, I would always drift off to a peaceful sleep.

Twigs and leaves crunched and snapped under our feet as the three of us continued to walk along the rim. It was getting colder.

"Let's see," Jared began to answer my question. "Mom always told us how much she loved us. She smothered us with love."

"Smo-thered," Jarvis whispered.

"She always told us how smart we were, especially Jarvis."

Stopping dead in his tracks and pointing toward the inky black horizon above the Canyon, Jarvis suddenly proclaimed, "This is it!"

"What? We're going out there? In the dark? Really?" I could not hide my shock.

Jarvis had stopped at the head of a trail that would walk us right out onto a point inside the Canyon. It was narrow with steep drop offs on either side. To make matters even more frightening, there was no moon to illuminate the path, and the wind was gusting up.

Not waiting for Jared and me, Jarvis started out on his own.

"Are you going to just let him walk out there?" I grabbed ahold of Jared's arm. I ducked as a bat swooped down above our heads.

"He'll be fine. Are you going to be OK?"

"I don't think I can do this."

"Now, where are those words of encouragement you're supposed to be speaking into yourself?"

"Well, you're not supposed to speak words that will make you do something foolish."

"And coming out west all alone and hanging out with two guys you've never met before isn't foolish? It doesn't sound like you needed a lot of encouragement to get this far."

"No. The first part, coming out west, I had to do. The second part, meeting up with you guys, you made easy."

I gazed out toward the point. Jarvis was nowhere to be seen, and Jared adamantly talked me through his options.

"Listen, Angie, I have to go out there to get Jarvis and I only have two options when I get there. One, you come with me, and the three of us can stargaze. Or two, you stay here, I bring him back, which won't be easy, and all three of us walk back to the cabins."

"I can walk myself back."

"Like hell you can! You may have come out here on your own, but I'll be damned if I'm going to let you walk back through the woods, on the rim, in the dark, and by yourself. Not on my watch." Jared crossed his arms signaling that he was standing firm. "Now make up your mind, because either way, I have to go out there, now."

"OK, I'm going with you." *This is nuts.*

"Good. Take my hand if you get scared. There's nothing to worry about." Something small rustled through the brush near my feet and made me jump. *Great.*

Jared and I began our walk out to Bright Angel Point. The first half of the trail was not too bad. There was a natural rock wall that wound around on our right side. Hugging that wall, I took Jared's hand and stayed right behind him. For my sake, Jared walked slow and steady.

"How are you doing back there?"

"Fine. I'm OK."

His hand was warm and strong. I scuffed a stone under my foot causing me to misstep. I felt Jared's grip tighten around mine.

"You're OK."

We rounded a corner and the rock wall disappeared. The next stretch was open on both sides. From what I could see in the dark, the path was only three to four feet wide. The drop on either side was straight down.

"It might be better if you do this on your own. Go across in front of me and I'll keep an eye on you."

"Right, so you can watch me fall to my death."

"You're not going to fall."

"You don't know that."

"You're right, I don't. And I can't promise that you won't. But I can promise that I'll die trying to prevent you from falling. How's that?"

"Not good enough."

"So, what now? Are you going to turn back?

"Jared, I have a fear of heights. This sort of thing petrifies me."

"So? I have a fear of... of..." Looking for something that he could claim as a phobia to match or better mine, Jared scanned the dark surrounding us. "I'm afraid of you."

"Me?"

"Yes. You. You scare the living daylights out of me. And, if I was your fiancé, I'd be out here on a plane tomorrow to either finish the trip with you, or take you home."

His sincere concern for my wellbeing overwhelmed me. If we had not been standing on a ledge, I may have had the urge to hug him or stroke his arm. He was the very thing that I feared, too. I knew I was enjoying my time with him way too much. I had looked forward to seeing him that night, but I was not ready to question or face my motives.

"OK. For you, and for Jarvis, I am going to do this."

I moved out in front of Jared, took a deep breath, and started out across the very narrow rock formation high above the darkened canyon. As I reached the halfway point, the wind gusted up and blew my hair across my face. I stopped to brush it aside.

"Are you OK, Angie?" Jared called out from somewhere behind me.

"I'm good." I started up again and soon reached a man-made bridge that crossed a small chasm in the rock. Thank God, the bridge had side rails. On the other side of the bridge, I stepped onto a large boulder that overlooked the Canyon. *I made it!* Waiting for us, Jarvis was standing on the far edge.

"Glad you could make it," he observed nonchalantly. As we came up behind him, Jarvis did not turn to look at either one of us. Jared and I carefully bumped shoulders in solidarity and chuckled. *I was glad we made it, too!*

I had conquered my fear. My stomach did a flip in ecstatic victory. I tried to look up at the sky, but the expanse of galaxies spread out above us made me dizzy.

Jared spread the blankets out. Jarvis laid down on the first one letting us to know that he had claimed it for himself. Jared indicated that I could share his.

Staring up into the night sky was like gazing into the history of the universe. There we were, stretched out on a large boulder overlooking a canyon that was formed billions of years ago. We gazed up and studied the infinite amount of stars that were thousands of light years away. At the time they were formed, our present state was just a point on their future continuum.

It was the most astounding thing I had ever seen or contemplated.

There were no words.

CHAPTER SEVEN

MATHIEU

"Who are those guys?" I had my cell phone on speaker as I brought up the pictures Garrison was streaming back to my laptop. I was having a bad night. I was OK with Angelica's call at 1:00 AM. However, Garrison's call at 2:30 AM left me in a state of great unrest.

"I knew you'd ask, so I did a little background check. The one lying on the blanket next to Angelica is Jared Lawson. He's 31, divorced, and works at Atlantic Yachts Inc., in Egg Harbor, New Jersey.

A 31-year-old divorcé was sharing a blanket with my fiancée? My eyes fixated on them. Garrison continued talking.

"Wait, wait. Back up." I had missed what he had just said.

"I said the other guy is his brother, Jarvis Lawson. He's 22, single, and unemployed.

"How does she know these guys?"

"Judging from their conversations, they've just met."

What? I did not know if that was a good thing, or a bad thing.

"What are they doing out in the middle of nowhere, in the total dark, and after midnight?" I hated to even ask. More than that, I was dreading the answer. But if there was anyone to deliver me the bad news, I wanted it to be Garrison. With him I knew it would go no further, and he would not attach judgment.

"It appears they're stargazing. The younger brother sounds like he is quite versed on the constellations. He's the one that led them to that spot."

"Dear God, Garrison, this is ripping me apart."

"Do you want me to bring her home?"

"No. In fact, can you stay out there for a while longer? Tonight she told me that she's going to extend her vacation. Now I know why."

Garrison responded with only a simple, "Yes. I'll stay on it."

That night I lay in bed alone with my nightmare unfolding before me while Angelica lay under the stars with two men I knew nothing about, and apparently, neither did she.

I called Garrison back.

"I want to know everything there is to know about those guys. I want a full report on my desk in the morning. I don't care who you have to get out of bed to get it done. And Garrison, are you packing?"

"Yes, sir."

"Well, you know what to do if you need to."

"Of course."

"And Garrison, don't leave her. She's my world. I can't lose her."

ANGIE

"Andromeda turned the world on its head. Well, at least Cassiopeia's world," Jarvis spouted out rather randomly.

"Who's Cassiopeia?" I asked.

"Cassiopeia was Andromeda's mother, and she bragged about Andromeda's beauty." Jarvis had actually answered me. Excitedly I realized that we might share another short conversation.

"Did Andromeda's beauty live up to her mother's boasts?" I was intrigued.

"Oh, yes. Look at her." Jarvis stretched out his right arm and pointed to a magnificent array of stars. She was a spiral galaxy suspended above an invisible horizon.

"Andromeda," he whispered.

MATHIEU

I tossed and turned the entire night. She was out there, somewhere under the stars, with two men she barely knew.

Were they friends, acquaintances?

Was this a planned getaway so she could be with someone she had known in her past? I do not believe that kind of lie is in her.

Could this be a wild side of her that I had not discovered in our three months of forever?

Were they the reason she had suddenly decided to stay longer than originally planned?

Garrison sounded sure that she had just met them within the past several days. He assured me that she was still wearing our ring, and it did not appear as though anything more than stargazing was going on. He called me again 30 minutes later to let me know that neither one of the men had a criminal record. I was sure he was hoping that the added information would help put my mind at ease. I knew I would receive his full report by morning.

I checked my laptop at 6:30 AM, and sure enough a complete report plus several more photos were awaiting me. As expected, Garrison's investigation was thorough.

Jared Mathers Lawson, the older brother, had graduated from MIT, magna cum laude, with a degree in mechanical engineering. He was currently employed by Atlantic Yachts, Inc., located in Egg Harbor, New Jersey. During his short time there, he had risen to the position of department head. He sounded like a smart guy, but apparently not smart enough. He married shortly after he was hired and then divorced seven years later. Garrison noted that Jared Lawson's wife ran off with one of their best male friends.

Mr. Lawson was an average looking guy: brown hair, brown eyes, 5'10" tall, about 190 lbs., and had all of his teeth. (I think Garrison added that last detail to humor me.) *Very funny, Garrison. I am not amused.* There was nothing else in his report on Jared Mathers Lawson worth a remark.

Jarvis Mathers Lawson, the younger brother, was another story. He resembled his older brother in many ways. He had the same brown hair and eyes. He was 5'9" tall and weighed 187 lbs. In his picture, and like his brother, he appeared to be physically fit. He graduated high school and had taken several classes at West Chester University centering on astronomy and meteorology. He still lived at home in West Chester, Pennsylvania. He was autistic. Garrison added his own note stating that Jarvis's autism may have explained some of the behavior and interactions, or lack thereof, he had observed. While Jarvis Lawson had no criminal record, highlighted in Garrison's report were notes made about altercations Jarvis had had in high school with fellow classmates and a PE teacher. Jarvis Lawson was currently seeing a therapist, Dr. Benjamin Conner Rush. He was also taking medication to treat his anxiety and anger.

Over the phone, Garrison assured me that everything seemed benign between the three, and he did not feel there was reason to be concerned about anyone's motives. He said the notes regarding Jarvis's high school incidents of assault did raise some red flags, but it had happened years ago, and Jarvis may have been bullied. He promised me that he would remain undercover and stay close to Angelica to guarantee her safety.

After we hung up, I stared at the picture they had taken on the South Rim and sent home to their mother, Mrs. Clara Mathers Lawson. The three of them were posed proudly overlooking the Grand Canyon on the Bright Angel Trail. Angelica, my future wife, looked so cute in her hiking boots, backpack strapped to her voluptuous body, her hair tucked up into her safari hat, and sporting a big smile as she practically laid her head on Jared Lawson's shoulder. Her dimples told me that she was at her best: free and amused by her new friends. Jared Lawson had his arm around her shoulder. A jealous ache tightly clamped my chest. I wanted to reach into the photo and cut off his arm. His smile was that of a man pleased with himself. I hated Jared Mathers Lawson at that moment, a moment that had taken place days ago and may have escalated to more than just friends in his mind.

"SHE'S ENGAGED!" I shouted at the picture that occupied the entire screen of my laptop.

Jarvis stood alone leaving a space between him and the other two. He was looking down at the ground. It was difficult to read anything about him from the picture, except that he was disconnected.

I took one last lingering gaze to study Angelica's face. She looked so happy.

CHAPTER EIGHT

JARED

In the morning, we planned to drive out to Cape Royal Trail and then hike the half-mile out to Angels' Window. By afternoon, we would be on our way to Zion Canyon and to what I believed would be the highlight of our trip. Angie told us last night that she was definitely in and extending her own vacation.

"Wow, your fiancé isn't concerned about your being out here by yourself?" I was shocked that it was that easy for her to change plans.

"No. Why should he be? I think he was disappointed, but he understands."

"Angie, honestly, I'm not sure I would understand. If I had a girl… uh, fiancée like you, I would not want her traveling the country by herself. What you're doing is highly irresponsible." I could not believe those words just blurted right out of my mouth like I was her father or older brother, someone that cared. "But if you're that determined to do this, I'm glad you've decided to hang with us rather than go off by yourself."

"Thanks. I think that's a vote of support?"

"No. It's just an invitation to continue hanging out with us. I would worry if you just went out on your own, even though I couldn't stop you if you did."

We walked in silence for a few yards and then Angie asked my brother a direct question.

"Jarvis, what do you think?"

"I think you need to go home."

"Jarvis!" I scolded him. "Don't be rude."

"She asked what I thought and I told her. Do you want me to lie?"

"You know," Angie jumped back in, "maybe he's right. This is supposed to be your vacation. I just kind of showed up and horned my way in."

"Horned! Now that's funny! *Horned,*" Jarvis repeated. He had found a new word that he liked. Ugh. Already he was wearing me out, and it was only 8:30 in the morning.

"Listen, Angie, are you going to Zion Canyon this afternoon?"

"Yes."

"Then stay with us. If you don't, I'll worry, and THAT would ruin our vacation."

"It won't ruin mine." Jarvis added his two cents. He was on a roll.

"I don't know. I'll think about it."

Angie was unusually quiet during our hike out to Angels' Window. I feared she was pondering her afternoon plans, so I was careful not to interrupt her thoughts. When we reached our destination, her spark returned. She quietly noted how incredible she thought the view was. We took pictures of the Colorado River as seen through the natural arch and then hiked out across the top. There was no one else out on that long spit of rock except the three of us. We just stood in wonder as the Canyon opened up below us. It seemed Angie had conquered her fear of heights.

I stood back and watched her take it all in. The wind blew through her hair as she closed her eyes, stretched out her arms, and inhaled deeply. Tasting the cool breeze that had swirled through the conifers of the North Rim, she smiled. She was such a free spirit. I knew then that she was going to strike out on her own, again.

ANGIE

I really can't say why I decided to stay longer.

"Because I wanted to?" That made me sound like a brat.

"Because I could?" That made me sound like a spoiled brat.

"Because I needed to?" That made me sound like a suffering spoiled brat, which was probably closest to the truth.

Was that reason enough? Was it because I was not ready to go home and start planning for what I was sure would be the wedding of the century? From whom was I running? My parents? His parents? Mathieu?

Why I decided to split off from the guys was a little more complicated. To stay would have meant that I was selfish enough to put my needs before someone else's. Jarvis had made it clear that I was barging in on his time with his older brother. Plus, I was becoming attached. I was beginning to care too much.

MATHIEU

Garrison sent footage of their departure from the North Rim. Angelica, the kind soul that she was, hugged the men good-bye. Well, she hugged one of them. The younger one resisted her advances. Garrison said he could tell that the older brother was clearly upset with Angelica and tried to convince her to stay with them and continue on to Zion. Otherwise, he strongly advised that she go home. According to my "fly on the wall," Jared Lawson had cautioned her, "It's not safe for you to be out here alone."

Jared seemed like a pretty nice guy, except I was beginning to think that he had developed feelings for my particularly sweet and sometimes naïve fiancée. Who could blame him? Spend fifteen minutes with Angelica and you would fall for her, too. Her smile could light up the night sky, and her spirit could lift the heaviest weight from your overburdened shoulders. Plus, she was smoking hot.

I prayed she would take Jared Lawson's advice and come home. It had been almost a week since she had left and I was missing her terribly. Since the first day we met, we had never been apart for more than 24 hours, I saw to that. Even when I was away on business, I would rush right back to her.

I remember inhaling the traces of fruit and honey in her hair when I would first seize her in my arms. She would bury her head into my right shoulder as my embrace closed around her waist. We wouldn't rush to kiss. She would allow me to cradle her, and we would gently sway as I whispered how much I loved and missed her. She was my sun and my moon, and when I could wait no longer, I would lift her chin and look deep into her crystal blue eyes. Her pout would begin to spread and break into a smile that prompted her dimples to make their reappearance. Then I could see and feel her deep contentment in the moment. Brushing my hand across the smooth skin of her face, I would caress her lips with mine. Wanting to take her completely, desire would surge through me.

I waited for her longer than for any other. Angelica was not a girl you rushed into. She was like the last rose bud remaining on the vine: delicate, tight, and too beautiful to tarnish. I know that most would find it hard to believe, but I did not spend the night with her until she initiated it.

Camille, her overly enthusiastic roommate, was away for the weekend. It was after midnight, and I was confused about whether to stay or go. We had not talked about it, and I did not know if it would be too forward to invite myself to stay the night. The rise and fall of our kisses and the journey of our hands made it fairly clear that our play was just beginning. Rising to leave the room in a soft flurry of unspoken sensual promises, Angelica quietly excused herself.

I will never forget it. I was sitting on her couch watching the movie credits roll by when she descended the stairs from her room. She was wearing a negligee that cupped her breasts and held them suspended by two thin straps. The fabric flowed across the curve of her hips and flared around her thighs. The gardens in heaven paled in comparison to her when she walked over and stood before me. Taking my face in her hands, I knew the night would belong to us. As she lowered her lips over mine, my hands slid from her thighs up to her breasts. My body reveled at her perfect skin as my fingers made their ascension. She pulled back and caused me to stand. Then she led me up the stairs to her bed.

The memory of her, all of her, and the thought of losing her brought tears to my eyes. The week had been too much for me to take like a man. She had reduced me to a lovesick boy, stripped of my pride, and desperately needing more than just her sultry voice over the phone. I knew I had become addicted.

"Please, Angel, come home..."

Camille called me, which she had never done before, and expressed her concern about Angelica's decision to stay out west longer than she had first planned. Looking for her only daughter, Angelica's mother called an hour later. She wanted to begin making appointments with visit several bridal salons in New York City. Mrs. Havens went on about taking the train, shopping, and having a late lunch before heading back. Her voice faded in my head as she rattled on about other ceremonious specifics that were not of immediate concern to me.

"I'll have her back by six," her mother assured me.

"Good luck with that," I felt like saying.

JARED

On the drive back to the cabins, Angie announced that she had decided it was time to part ways. That was not exactly what she said, but it was exactly what she meant.

"Are you going home?" I felt at that point in our acquaintance I had the right to ask.

"No, I think I'll head out to Bryce first, and then I'll head for home."

She looked down at her hands, wringing them in her lap as she spoke. I could tell that was not what she wanted to do; it was what she thought she had to do.

Damn you, Jarvis. You caused this. You made her feel like an imposition. Those were my first thoughts. I was really mad at my brother for always being so damned honest and not being able to filter his thoughts before he spoke. He could be so cold sometimes.

"Angie, you have my number. Keep it. If you get into any trouble, you call me. Don't even hesitate or think twice about it. If I read about you in the paper or see your face as a headline story, I will be devastated."

Jarvis snorted. My patience with him was running thin.

After she had packed, she began bringing her luggage out onto the porch shared by our cabins.

"Come on, Jarvis. You should at least come out and say good-bye," I summoned.

To my surprise, he followed me without a fight.

The three of us stood and stared at her luggage that she had parked neatly outside her door.

"Ready to go?" I asked.

"Yep, this is it. It's been great hiking with you guys, riding the mules, and especially the stargazing. Thanks."

Angie leaned in to give Jarvis a hug. His radar was on high alert for just that sort of thing. He immediately backed away. Angie looked at me. I shook my head furtively to let her know that it would be best not to pursue him. Then much to my surprise, Jarvis looked up, his eyes actually met hers, and he spoke.

"I'm sorry for what I said, Miss Angelica Orabelle Havens."

Angie, God bless her, rushed him and held him in her arms as his body twitched uncomfortably. He was a giant compared to her. Watching their moment cautiously, I began to relax as I slowly came to trust that he was not going to shove or strike her. After the initial contact and shock, Jarvis loosened up and actually allowed his arms to encircle her own.

I felt emotion well up within my chest. I cannot tell you whether it was because Angie was leaving us, or because Jarvis had apologized, accepted, and reciprocated an embrace - *her embrace.*

Dragging her largest piece of luggage behind me, I walked Angie out to her car. The afternoon sun had warmed up the pavement under our feet, and when she opened the trunk of her car, the heat escaping it reminded me of our struggle to climb back up the Bright Angel Trail on the South Rim. It was one of those challenges that showed us what we were made of, and I had learned that Angie was made of steel. Watching her interact with Jarvis over the past several days also let me know that she was full of compassion and patience.

"You can change your mind, you know," I said as I closed the trunk.

"I know. But, I can't. Thanks for everything, Jared. I'm really going to miss you and Jarvis. You guys are the best."

"You're not so bad yourself," I said giving her a little love punch to her shoulder, and then before I knew what I was doing, I pulled her in for a hug.

"Mr. Dufour is the luckiest man on earth. He must be one hell of a guy," I whispered into her hair.

"Yes..." She said into my shoulder. I felt her voice move through my body.

"Angie, hold on to my number. Call me if you need me." I had lost my mind. I was going to say things I knew I should never say to one who was already promised. If there was anything I had learned in my miserable marriage, it was that you would always regret what you did not say more than what you did.

I took her hands in mine and held her at arms length so I could speak directly to her. "I wish you would change your mind and travel with us. It won't be the same without you. I've grown fond of your smile, and..." Her eyes turned a softer blue and her smile disappeared. This was not easy for her, either. "... Jarvis really does like you. I have never in my life seen him accept a hug or offer an apology. He needs you, too."

I had just implicated that I needed her first, and maybe I did.

I remember watching her drive away.
"Turn around, dammit. TURN AROUND!"

Just like that, Angelica Orabelle Havens had left a deep imprint on my life and Jarvis's life, too.

~

The drive to Zion Canyon was long, hot, and lonely. Just as I had done during our caravan to the North Rim, I kept looking in the rearview mirror hoping that Angie's car would fall in behind us. After an hour or more of that, I resigned myself to the fact that she was on her way to Bryce and was now miles away. I also bucked up and told myself that I needed to begin exercising some self-control. After all, this trip *was* supposed to be about Jarvis and me. It was our reunion tour. It was our time to bond.

I had known Jarvis for 22 years, and never once had he allowed me to hug him. Angie knew him for a mere five days, and he received and reciprocated her affection.

Along the way, she had stolen my heart. The pain I felt was real.

CHAPTER NINE

JARED

Praise God! The beds in our Zion cabin were facing north! I had been working hard all day to focus on Jarvis and give him my full attention. I had prepared myself for what awaited us on the other side of that cabin door. To my great relief, I had found a small sanctuary rather than a chaotic undertaking. It was a far better ending to a miserable drive.

As we sat down to dinner at the Red Rocks Grill in the Zion Lodge, my thoughts turned to Angie. Studying the menu, I saw several selections that I thought Angie would have enjoyed. I ordered an entrée salad. Angie would have been proud. When it was delivered to our table, I was sorry that she was not there to share it with me. I could picture her picking out the onions and laying them neatly on her butter plate. She would have requested a balsamic vinaigrette dressing. I requested the same. Jarvis ate his steak quietly. Without Angie there, we dined in silence. I gazed out the window and watched a family hauling their luggage out of their van and into the lodge lobby. I wanted to call Angie to make sure she had arrived safely at Bryce, but decided it was inappropriate to just casually call someone else's fiancée. He was the one that should have been worried, not me. I ordered the chocolate lava cake for dessert.

Who is he? Why isn't he out here chasing her down?

Their relationship was none of my affair, although I was tempted to make it one.

I was excited for our hike on the floor of Zion Canyon the next day. But admittedly, I knew it would also

be dampened by Angie's absence. I had no idea what
Jarvis was feeling. He seemed content with his steak.

JARVIS

I had to wear those stupid boots that hurt my feet.
You have to wear socks with those boots. My socks
bothered me. They had a seam that dug into my toes. I had
to lace up my boots. The laces bothered me. Jared told me
to stop complaining or he was going to leave me behind. I
wished he had. I wished he had stayed behind, too.

Then I had to fill my bladder, the one in my
backpack.

"Blad-der."

Jared said, "Shut up."

I was so sick of stupid hiking rules. I poured spring
water into the bladder. But I was going to have a lot of pee
in my real bladder if I drank all of that water, and then I
would have to pee in the river. When we were growing up,
Jared showed me how to pee all over the place.

"Pee!"

"Jarvis! Cut the crap and get busy."

Jared said "crap."

"Crap!"

Jared was annoyed. He handed me the stupid hiking
pole. I did not know why he thought I needed it. I knew
how to walk.

"Stu-pid."

We boarded a bus that took us to the Temple of
Sinawava.

"Sin-a-wa-va."

Jared said that was where we would find the River
Walk trailhead. The bus driver had a microphone and he
said that "Sinawava" referred to the Coyote God of the
Paiute Indians.

"Pai-u-te"

The Paiute Indians believed that the coyote was a trickster. I liked that, too.

"Trick-ster"

The best part was when the bus driver said the name of the river was "The Virgin River." I laughed out loud. Jared told me to shut up.

"Virgin. Oooooooo!"

I could tell Jared was getting ready to physically silence me. So, I stopped.

As we struck out on our mile-long hike alongside the Virgin River, I named all of the virgins I could think of.

"Virgin Airlines
Virgin Gorda
Virgin Islands
Virgin Mary
Virgin Olive Oil
The Virgin Queen"

"Would you please shut up about it?" Jared barked at me. At least he asked that time.

"Vir-gin-ya" (Heavy accent on the last syllable.)

I like having the last word.

JARED

I was very close to leaving Jarvis behind, even if it meant I would have to stay behind with him. The whole Virgin River and backpack bladder thing was sending him into one of his tailspins. I was really beginning to have my doubts about his ability to keep it together on the long hike up the river. I decided if he lost control, I would turn around and take him back to the lodge. If that happened, it would prove Mom was right; Jarvis was not ready to face the world on his own. At that moment, I was having my doubts, too.

The signs at the trailhead told us to make sure we stopped to appreciate the flora and fauna along the way. Good advice. I had heard hikers before us say that Zion Canyon was by far the best part of the Grand Circle Tour. The different elevations, water supply, and varying temperatures had spawned many riparian and aquatic ecosystems. The numerous waterfalls seeping through the Navajo sandstone cliffs along the Virgin River supported lush hanging gardens, cottonwood trees, and ferns.

Zion's rustic environment and serene setting had a calming effect on Jarvis. He took out his iPhone, and as we continued our hike together, Jarvis took some great pictures of our surroundings. He even snapped off a few of me. I planned to take some of him and send them home to Mom, and maybe Angie, too.

I stopped and waited while Jarvis tried to zero in on a tree that appeared to have a small spring emanating from its exposed roots. It was a little sapling whose seed had germinated just a foot off the path. Water coming down the opposite cliff had found its way beneath the footpath to reemerge and bubble up at the base of the happy sprig. The sound of the trickling spring and Jarvis's inner peace finally put me at ease. I allowed my thoughts to drift. Angie had texted me the night before to let me know that she had made it safely to her "destination" and asked how we were doing. I replied that our trip was quiet, and that we had found our cabin in good order. She responded that she was glad to hear that we were OK and wanted us to know that she had arrived safe and sound. She thanked me again for a "great experience" at the Grand Canyon and wished us well. I wondered if she had found another person or persons to tag along with at Bryce. I had mixed feelings about that. If she took up with another group of people, would she forget about us? Would she ever give me another thought? If she did not find another group to travel with, would she be putting herself at risk? *Where is this Mathieu guy? Why is he allowing her to do this?*

That is the funny thing about memories. Even though they are made together, you're never quite sure if everyone involved will treasure or hold on to them in the same way. I knew I would never forget Angie. However, I did not know if she would ever think about us again. One day she would marry and become Mrs. Mathieu Dufour, probably have a gaggle of beautiful children, and live happily ever after.

Will she be happy?

She deserved to be happy.

How sad if her dimples were extinguished forever in the wake of hurt and disappointment.

I prayed she would never know the pain I felt when I found Erin and Blaine in my bed. I was devastated. Worse yet, it was clear that my ex-wife was the seducer. I did not want to believe that it was Blaine who was under her. They were so lost in each other; they did not know I was standing in the doorway. Their next thrust made my nightmare undeniable. I roared.

"GET THE HELL OUT OF MY BED!"

I wanted to run at them and tear them apart. But the sight of their naked bodies writhing together repulsed me. I had no desire to touch their damp sweaty skin generated by their filth and disloyalty. At the sound of my voice, Blaine peered around the curve of my wife's heart-shaped bottom he had clutched in his hands. He sat up erect as Erin yanked the sheet over their bodies.

"Get the fuck out of my house before I kill you, you son of a bitch!" I am sure I was shaking. In that moment, I wanted to kill my best friend since grade school.

He got out of my bed, grabbed his clothes, and tried to cover up what I had seen in our high school locker room on numerous occasions, but never before had it been filled with lusty desire for my wife.

How long has this been going on?

A string of obscenities flowed from my mouth and followed him out my bedroom door.

"Get dressed." I slammed the door on my sobbing wife.

I prayed that Angie's fiancé would never hurt her like that. I prayed she would keep my cell number. I knew I would always keep hers.

Memories. We all share them. Some we would like to delete permanently like an old email, and the good ones we would like to keep as a screensaver for life. However, you can never delete an email permanently, can you? It is always out there waiting to be dug up. Bad memories are like that. They dance on the periphery of our good times and wait for someone with malicious intent to stumble upon them.

Angie could have easily been my beautiful screensaver for life.

I could appreciate why Angie bolted, (my word, not hers.) She was a free spirit. Why would she want to be dragged down by my issues? I had lived most of my life allowing my plans to be directed by someone else. Perhaps that was part of what drove Erin into another man's arms. It seemed my whole childhood, and to a large extent my adult years, had been dictated by Jarvis's needs or moods. (Jarvis would tell you he did not have moods, but I knew different.) My guilt and sympathy for him reigned over me.

I chose my station at Jarvis's side. Mom had told me repeatedly that even though we were a family team, I did not have to include Jarvis in everything I did. She constantly reminded me that I was not his primary caregiver, nor should I feel responsible for him all of the time.

Originally, she had encouraged me to take the Grand Circle Tour with a group of friends. Jarvis cried "Unfair!" and I begged her to let him come along. Perhaps I needed to let go more than she did.

It occurred to me that maybe I was meant to meet Angie. She was running from captivity. I was always running toward it. It was an intersection waiting to happen. I hoped her life as Mrs. Dufour would turn out better than Erin's life had as Mrs. Lawson. Maybe Jarvis had it right. Maybe Looser-son was more appropriate.

After the first mile and rounding the next bend, the dry trail vanished into the river. We had reached The Narrows, and it was time to get wet. Preparing for their descent into the water, a group of college-aged students were gathered around the entry point. They were removing their outer layers and stuffed anything they intended to keep dry into their backpacks. Brandishing their bare chests that appeared waxed and buffed for just such an occasion, the guys stripped off their shirts. The girls did not bother to feign modesty as they revealed a variety of bikini tops of multiple shapes and sizes. *Talk about topography and the lay of the land!* I told myself not to stare. It had been a long time...

I was envious of their co-ed camaraderie. I had many friends when I was in college. However, when they chose to take their treks during our winter and spring breaks, I chose to return home to spend time with Mom and Jarvis. When we were all reunited back at school, I was subjected to listening to their tales of conquest, which became more risqué with each subsequent trip.
The eventual split between Erin, Blaine, and me demanded that our friends choose between us. Many of them chose "none of the above."

Jarvis and I dropped our backpacks to the ground, pulled our shirts over our heads, and stuffed them into our packs. We headed into the numbing cold water of the Virgin River.
It is believed, but not certain, that the river was named "La Virgen" by Spanish Catholic Missionaries in

honor of the Virgin Mary. Jarvis could not handle that for several reasons.

First, he did not believe in God. If it was not tangible, if it could not be spelled out in black and white, particularly if it had no numeric significance to support its claim, then it was highly unlikely that Jarvis could give it any credence. He would not allow faith to own a slot in his tool set. He believed Jesus once walked the earth, and he had no doubts about Jesus' role as a great prophet. But, as the Son of God? That was pure malarkey to him. He would tell you straight up that all of the gods were nothing short of myth to help people blame their shortcomings on something other than themselves. He made it clear that man created the gods because man's greatest failings needed to be justified by something or someone greater than himself. Therefore, the gods, having had ultimate control, absolved man of all responsibility. Jarvis rarely pontificated about much, but he was certain about the irrational belief system man had invented for his own sanctification and sanity.

Mom and I, on the other hand, learned to lean on our faith. As Jarvis's obsessions and idiosyncrasies became more difficult to navigate, I was becoming old enough to understand the meaning and importance of having a spiritual life. Mom would give me hope by explaining that we didn't know God's plan for Jarvis; however, she was certain that He had one and that we were privileged to be a part of it.

I grew envious of friends that had brothers who were closer in age and without "issues." Mom was swift to correct me.

"Jarvis doesn't have issues. He has unique gifts. He may not allow you to wrestle him, and he may not want to talk about the same things your friends do, but there is a reason you love him so much. Tell me why you love your brother?"

Mom had a way of turning my biggest questions back to me for answers. Once I asked her why God made

Jarvis the way he was. She listened intently as I tried to answer that one for myself. Because I had asked that question many times throughout the years, I knew I would eventually reach the same conclusion that centered on the same basic truth; Jarvis had a brilliant mind giving him a unique place in the world. He would never cease to amaze us.

Here is another truth. Human nature does not like "unique." We like everything to fit into a neat package that fits a norm that we invented so we can exercise some sense of control over it. The more control we have, the more comfortable we are. The more comfortable we are, the more we try to protect the neat package we invented. Jarvis spends much of his life outside the norm. He exceeds the norm, which makes others uncomfortable, and that is their failing.

When you think about it, Jarvis really is not all that different in many regards. He has a "norm." It is just different than ours, and he works very hard to protect it, just like everyone else. Sometimes, he makes me work very hard to protect his norm, too. My mother raised me to respect and adjust to the differences in others. It was not easy for us, but we counted ourselves blessed every day. Some days it was a little more difficult to feel blessed than others. However, when we took inventory, we both acknowledged that our exceptionally great days outnumbered our more difficult days, proving conclusively just how blessed we were beyond the social norm.

I loved my brother very much. And though he would never express it, I knew he loved me, too.

The Virgin River ran swift and opposed our direction. It pushed hard against our ankles and calves. I battled to keep my balance. Like everyone else ahead of us, we used our hiking poles to negotiate the rocks and navigate the depths of the menacing shallow whitewater. It gave me a real appreciation for the signs cautioning hikers to wear proper footwear and bring along a sturdy hiking pole. It took me several minutes to settle into the rhythm of the river. Jarvis, on the other hand, and surprisingly so, had no trouble. With his pack on his back and pole in hand, he was quickly pulling ahead of me. I had to suck it up and move on to stay with him. He showed no hesitation when it came to trudging through the resistance of the river's current and the confrontation posed by the submerged rocks.

When we had left the lodge in the morning, the skies were clear, and a park ranger assured us that we would not see rain that day. "… just like every other day this month," he added. It looked like he'd gotten it right.

The walls of the canyon had to be 300-500 feet straight up. They blocked the sun like a thick forest canopy. About a half hour into our hike up the river, the rising sun crested the east rim, and the canyon began heating up. The thin slice of sky above us was a deep royal blue: a patriotic blue as ever there was one. The color reminded me of Angie's eyes. The water was crystal clear, and the river rocks were visible for the most part. Thankfully, we were able to strategically place each foot in our forward progress. Reducing our world to the narrowing path before us, variegated salmon-colored sandstone cliffs towered overhead and trapped the heat.

Several hours up the river, we stopped for a snack. We had found a dry sandy spot to unload the weight on our backs and sit down. There was a small pool of water opposite our meager makeshift port that was deep enough for a swim. I watched as a family of four children splashed and played "chicken fight."

It must be nice to have siblings to climb on your back and wrestle like that. They were entertaining, and I lived vicariously through their antics and banter as I ate my granola bar. Their parents sat several yards away taking pictures of their family in combat.

I will never have pictures like that to look back on.

In the Lawson family photo album, one could detect that Jarvis was pulling away from Mom and me as he grew older.

"I'm going for a swim before we head back," I announced to Jarvis who was busy writing a numeric sequence in the sand with a thin stick. He ignored me. Hoping they would dry quickly in the arid air, I removed my hiking shoes and placed them on a rock next to my backpack. I thought it possible that Jarvis did not hear me the first time.

"Jarvis, do you want to go for a swim before we start up again?"

"No."

I walked in without him. I was almost happy he had decided not to join me, keeping his bad attitude to himself. He was a man of few words, and sometimes when he was with me, it made me lonelier than if I were truly alone.

The riverbed dropped off suddenly and dumped me up to my chest in icy cold water. I let out a yelp that caused Jarvis to laugh uproariously. He thought it was the funniest thing he had ever seen. Normally, his reaction would have annoyed me. However, I knew that Angie would have been laughing right along with him. I could almost hear her sarcastic admonishment, and she would have left me with one option only: to pull her in with me. Thoughts of Angie put me in a playful mood, so I took a large swipe at the water and sent a sizable spray in Jarvis's direction.

"Hey, you moron!" Jarvis only called me names when he was really pissed. He grabbed his backpack, slung it over his shoulder, and started back toward the lodge. *"Here we go."* I frowned as my brother stomped off.

"Wait!" I climbed back up the riverbank where my pack was leaning up against a boulder and hopefully stayed dry.

I felt a small vibration under my feet, and I heard what I thought was thunder. But the rumble didn't stop, nor did the ground. In fact, it escalated into a roar that echoed off the canyon walls farther upstream. I recalled the signs we had seen at the trailhead.

CHAPTER TEN

JARED

"IT'S A FLASH FLOOD! RUN! UP THE ROCKS! GET
TO HIGH GROUND! GET OUT OF THE CANYON!" a man
ahead of us began shouting. As the noise grew louder and
the ground felt like it was moving under our feet, people
ran screaming from the water and began scurrying up the
rocks in a panic.
    "JARVIS, CLIMB! GO AS HIGH AS YOU CAN! GO!
MOVE IT!" With his backpack hanging off his shoulder, he
began climbing up the boulders and rocks that formed the
canyon wall. My heart was pounding as I prepared for the
first wave to strike. It was not yet in sight, but it was
approaching rapidly. I looked back for the children. They
were being dragged out of the water by their parents. Then
I noticed a woman running up stream toward me.
    "JARED! WHAT'S HAPPENING?"

Angie...?

    "ANGIE, COME ON! RUN!" I called out to her. But
she could not hear me above the commotion of people and
the roar that was growing louder and sucking up the
canyon airspace. She was going to be swept away. I looked
for Jarvis. He was making his way up. He had found a
crevice with enough crags and rocks to climb steadily up.
    There are no words to describe what happened next.
I did not think about it. I acted irrationally. Some would
say foolishly. Some might say heroically. I can tell you
none of that crossed my mind other than I had to get her
out of the water and up to higher ground.
    I ran back into the cold water.

"Angie! It's a flash flood. We have to go!" I reached for her arm and viciously pulled her out of the water and up the first rock. I heard her scream, probably in pain, but I also heard waves of water crashing down the canyon just above the bend.

"Angie, come on. You're going to drown us both if you don't move it!" I felt her beginning to advance under her own power. She was not moving fast enough, so I continued pulling. I saw another hand wrap around her other arm. It was Jarvis. He had come back.

Jarvis directed us up a path of smaller rocks that offered a quicker climb. It could not have been more than several seconds later that we saw the massive wall of murky water racing downstream toward us. It was claiming the canyon with a violent surge.

"Climb!" I yelled at both of them.

There was no denying the danger we were in and fear forced us to move harder and faster than I thought possible. Jarvis was leading the way. As the crevice narrowed, I moved to the rear. It appeared as though we would not make it high enough in time.

Oddly, I could no longer hear other voices. There were no screams or calling out of directions. *Where did everyone go?*

"Climb straight up and don't look down," I coaxed Jarvis and Angie. They had to keep moving.

Unfortunately, I did look down. Several of the students we had seen at the beginning of the river walk had lost their grip on a boulder they were clinging to and were immediately drug under by the current. I looked up and over to both sides with the hope of catching a glimpse of the family that had been playing in the water only minutes before. I remembered hearing the children cry and scream as their parents hauled them out of the water when it had all started. There were no signs of them. They were gone. My heart sank. *What if they didn't…?* I wanted to wail. There was no time to ponder or grieve. I would have to contain it and move on.

The first wall of water had moved well beyond us, but the water level remained exceedingly high behind it. Moving at an excessive rate of speed, it uprooted everything in its path and was shoving it down river toward the Temple of Sinawava. The beautiful and pristine Virgin River had turned muddy, full of tree limbs and brush, and was raging in her disgust. An innocent flip-flop was caught in the torrent of debris when it submerged below the surface in the same place I had last seen the students. It had all happened so fast, and it seemed our fate was likely doomed as well. We were racing a clock that knew no mercy and a tide that clearly had devastation on its mind.

My leg muscles were burning. My hands and feet were being scraped raw which reduced my ability to get a good grip. My will to survive kept demanding more from me as my body began to labor under the stress. My brother was a beast. Pulling Angie along with him, Jarvis continued his climb. Angie, on the other hand, was showing signs of distress. No doubt, without Jarvis's strength she would not have made it that far. As our pace began to slow from fatigue, I noticed fresh droplets of blood on the rocks and boulders ahead of me. One of them was bleeding.

Fortunately, we were gaining ground on the water.

Maybe it will level off.
Maybe this is as bad as it's going to get.

Believing the worst was over, I called up to Jarvis and suggested that he slow down. We needed to focus on our footing. Just yards below us, it seemed the water had halted its ascent; however, its velocity remained frightening. We needed to be more careful. If we slipped and fell, we would be swept away and drowned. All we needed to do was make it to the rim and climb out.

"Move straight up, Jarvis. Slow and steady."

"I know, I know." Jarvis was annoyed, but I was so proud of him. If any person were going to panic and not be able to handle a situation so out of control, I would have bet my last beer on Jarvis. Instead, he had rallied. He came back to get us. He pulled us out and led us up the canyon wall. I'm not sure Angie and I would have made it alone without his added brute force, fortitude, and uncanny sense of direction.

"Angie, are you OK?"

"I don't know." Following his hand grabs and footholds, she was doing her best to stay with Jarvis.

The climb was grueling. The threat of the river below us had fueled our initial shot of adrenaline. But I could feel myself tiring.

"I need to stop!" Angie panted.

We were on a long ledge and she was having trouble breathing. I examined her face and studied the water below us. I thought it better to let Angie catch her breath rather than push her too hard and risk a fall. We stopped for a breather on our hallowed ledge.

I looked for the source of blood that had left a distinct trail during our climb. It was coming from Jarvis's shins and calves. His legs were marred with gashes and scrapes from hauling Angie up the escape route that he had fortunately navigated for us to follow.

"Are you alright, Jar?" Blood covered the ankles and the heels of his hiking boots. He looked down and watched a crimson trickle follow the tail of his bootlace.

"I'm so sorry," Angie apologized, panting as she went to reach for his leg. Jarvis's faced filled with tense provocation. I grabbed her arm and pulled her back. I knew she only wanted to take a closer look and assess the severity of Jarvis's wounds. However, I could not risk his reaction to her touch, especially if he was in pain.

"We'll get him looked at as soon as we're out of here," I assured her.

"I'll survive." Jarvis took a long draw from his camelback, exhaled deeply, and sat back.

My bare feet were not much better. All three of us were pretty messed up.

"Jarvis, think you could spare some of that water for the rest of us?" I asked somewhat disappointed but not surprised that he had not offered it.

"No."

"What?"

"Germs."

"Jarvis, we don't have germs and we could really use it."

He did not move.

"Give it up, now!"

"It's all right, Jared. Leave him be. He saved us down there." Angie turned to Jarvis who was perched a few feet away. He refused to look up at her. "Thank you. Neither one of you had to come back for me," she added.

Jarvis grabbed his backpack and extended it out to us.

"Whoa! Not over the canyon!" If he had dropped it, it would have disappeared into the water below.

"Don't put your mouth on it," was Jarvis's one demand.

I held the pack up for Angie so the water would trickle out, and she did the same for me. Firmly pushing the water valve to the off position, I set the pack down and prepared myself to give Angie the full force of everything I had been holding back since I first saw her in the water. I was fueled by the loss of an innocent family who were undoubtedly swept away like the college students whose fate I had witnessed first hand. It terrified me to think that Angie could have been drowned along with them. I swiped my forearm across my mouth, and then I gave her an earful.

"Now, do you mind telling me what the hell you think you're doing here?"

The river continued to rage just below us, and I opened up.

"You could have killed all three of us. You're supposed to be at Bryce. What if I hadn't seen you? What then? Who would have known you were here? You could have been swept away. Is anyone else aware that you came to Zion rather than Bryce? Huh? What about your fiancé? Does he know where you are? What kind of a person neglects to tell her soon-to-be-husband that she's had a change of heart and has decided to stalk two guys into parts unknown? Who does that, Angie? Who? Is this a game to you? I invited you to stay with us. In fact, I *encouraged* you to stay with us. But, no, you couldn't do that. If you didn't want to be with us, if you didn't like hanging out with us, why didn't you just say so."

I was on a roll and building momentum.

"Instead, you chose to lie. You said you felt like you were "horning" in on our vacation and decided that it was best if you went on to Bryce. If you were horning in on our vacation, I would have told you." (That was *my* huge lie. I would have never said that. I was happiest when she was with us.) "Then you left us, only to return like some sort of stalker. Who does that, Angie? Who? Is this what you do for kicks? I would have never guessed that about you. I was really beginning to like you, a lot."

"JARED! Enough!" Jarvis scolded. "She heard you. Leave her alone."

I was stunned. Jarvis called me out. He stood up for Angie. He did have feelings. He had a heart. He possessed empathy.

With tears in her eyes, Angie gathered herself, stood to a crouching position, and tried to find a good foothold so she could put some distance between us.

"Wait!" I grabbed her arm. "I'm sorry. It's just that... well, if... if we had lost you, I would have died. I probably would have died trying to save you. Jarvis could have died trying to save you, and I don't think I could live with losing either one of you."

Angie sat back down and looked into my eyes saying nothing, just staring, probably searching for what I was trying my best to say. I took a different approach.

"Why *did* you come back?" I asked in a lowered tone.

Angie dropped her gaze and whispered to the rock ledge we were perched on.

"For the same reason you asked me to stay."

When I didn't respond, she raised her head. Angie's sapphire eyes clung to mine. I knew I should look away. I knew there was a man waiting for her back in Pennsylvania, and that a real hero would return her with her honor intact. I had to be that man, even though everything within me wanted to place my hands on her angelic face and kiss her lips. I just wanted to hold her. Fortunately, my moral upbringing kicked in, and I turned away from her. Our fate under the current conditions deserved my full attention.

The river had receded slightly and leveled off about fifty-yards below us. The murky water continued to race through the canyon, throwing a large mare's tail at the bend just up stream from our position. We were alone, just the three of us, perched high in the beauty and the hell of Zion Canyon.

MATHIEU

Garrison had called to let me know that Angelica, for reasons he could not explain, never made it to Bryce Canyon. Instead, she split left and took UT Rt. 9 - West. From there she proceeded to Zion National Park.

"Is she lost?" I asked Garrison, trying to conceal a wave of panic that was sweeping over me.

"No, I don't believe so. She knew exactly what she was doing."

Garrison explained that Angelica had made a deliberate turn to the west. Never once did her car slow down, nor did she appear to be fiddling with the GPS.

"Stay with her, Garrison. Don't lose her. I want to know her whereabouts and her intentions. Call me at the end of the day, or if she meets up with those guys again or anyone else for that matter."

JARED

Returning the camelback to Jarvis, I suggested that we keep moving toward the rim.

"OK, I'm ready." Angie took a deep breath, looked up to the sky for a glimpse of hope and started to stand up on her feet.

That was when I noticed the water swelling. Something had changed. The river was rising faster than any climb we could muster.

"Move it!"

Jarvis grabbed onto the next rock with one hand and pulled Angie with the other. I placed my left foot onto a boulder to the left and gave Angie's rear a shove up with my right shoulder. They were on the next ledge when I felt the swift current begin to pull at my ankles and then my calves. It was going to drag me under. I looked up. Jarvis was pulling Angie up onto the next foothold. She reached down and grabbed my shirt. The earth moved. I mean the earth literally moved. Rock and dirt began falling out from under me. It felt like I was being sucked into a vortex. I grabbed the branch of an errant tree above me and pulled myself up. It was a mistake; the branch was weak and began giving way. Angie, still precariously latched onto my shirt, tried to pull me higher. Jarvis reached down and grabbed a belt loop on my jeans. The shifting weight of his backpack almost threw him over my head. Somehow he managed to leverage himself, pull back, and give me enough momentum to throw my leg over and swing half of my body up and onto their ledge. As I hurled my weight up, I accidentally yanked Angie back against me.

As we lay there in our little collapsed heap, the roar of the rushing water began to fade out, and just as suddenly as it had all started, the river subsided and shrank back down into the canyon below us. Everything seemed to be settling when all at once the earth heaved. The boulders came alive and wanted to swallow us. The world as we knew it, the few square yards of visibility that we had, was going to crush and bury us, or throw us into the sinking water. Either way, we would all die from the fall, or drown.

"Come on!" Jarvis was the first to move as everything began shaking rapidly. Debris rained down on us as we crawled toward the opening Jarvis had found. He pulled Angie in first, but not without incident. Just as she was entering the mouth of a concealed cave, a large boulder sliced between us. It narrowly missed my head, but I heard a distinct snap as it clipped her leg. At first, I thought it dropped her into the canyon. My eyes searched for her and Jarvis. I could barely hear them over the rage of the mad canyon wall. First, I spotted Jarvis in the shadow of a dark cavernous space. Next to him, Angie peered out. I was relieved to know they had both made it to safety. I was not so fortunate. A large crack in the rock ledge had opened up, separating me from them.

As I tried to assess my options, there was another massive shift and deafening heave. Rock and dirt began careening down in a landslide that had been triggered somewhere above us. Jarvis and Angie disappeared in the dust. Their calls for me were lost in the thunderous roar of the death-dealing rockslide. Jarvis began screaming as if he were coming apart. I slid further in their direction knowing that one small boulder could take me down. Reaching as far forward as I could, Jarvis found my hand and pulled me through as I pushed off the ledge. I fell into the cave and on top of them. Dirt, rock, trees and anything else left on the canyon rim began to cover the opening of our small sanctuary. The cave was going to be covered over, and our tomb would be sealed.

The landslide continued as the earth rumbled like thunder and shook like an earthquake. The tremor made it impossible to move with any intent. The dust was thick and I could faintly hear Angie choking on it. Jarvis continued calling for me even though I was within feet of him. I waited for the ceiling of our small cave to give way.

"Cover your heads." I yelled.

"Zion means sanctuary," the shuttle driver announced to set the stage for his passengers before they disembarked for their inspiring river walk.

This is not a sanctuary. This is a hellhole. The three of us are going to die here today.

I thought about my mom and how she would miss us. Strangely, I thought about my dad.

Inexplicably, the ground stopped shaking and all I could hear were Angie's sobs, Jarvis gagging on whatever he had inhaled, and the pounding of my heart. Choking on the dust that hung in the polluted airspace encasing us, I tried to open my burning eyes. It was pitch black with the exception of one ray of light peering through a break in the rock above our heads. The radiant beam dramatically dimmed and disappeared whenever the wind outside blew a heavy gust of dust and debris across the only crack in our sepulcher.

"*1, 1, 2, 3, 5, 8, 13, 21...*" It was Jarvis. He was working to hold it together. He had the presence of mind to take control of himself.

"Angie, are you all right?" Lying in a heap within several feet of me, I could barely make out her figure.

"I think so, but I can't feel my foot." My hand went to reach for her limb, any limb, any part of her that would give me to know that she was breathing and OK. When I touched what I thought was her leg, she cried out in pain.

"Oh, dear God, that hurts! It's my ankle," she hissed through her teeth. Trying to endure the worst of it, she bit down and groaned.

"I'm so sorry. I didn't mean to hurt you." I had no idea how to comfort her at that moment.

"Jarvis, are you still with us?"

"Right here, Jared. Can you see me?" He coughed raggedly.

"Not really. It's so dark in here." I knew better than to try and reach out for him.

"34, 55, 89, 144 ..."

"Are you OK?" I asked again.

" I think so. This is not good, Jared."

"I know. Be quiet and see if we can hear anyone outside."

We sat still. Angie sucked in her breath. A few feet away from Angie and me, Jarvis sat silently with his legs pulled up in an upright fetal position. I did not dare move for fear that I might hurt Angie, again.

Nothing. We heard nothing, only the river below us and a steady drip from somewhere inside our entombed so-called sanctuary.

"Maybe we should all scream together and see if anyone outside can hear us."

"What? And cause another landslide?" Angie's fear was palpable.

"It's all we've got. If there's anyone nearby, we need to let them know we're here, now."

The three of us began screaming for help as loud as we could. Bouncing around the close interior walls of the cave, our cries for help were absolutely earsplitting. After several seconds, we stopped and listened. We tried three or four more times. Nothing. No one. We were alone.

Where did everybody go?

"Where is everyone?" Angie asked. "There were so many people around when this all started. Where did they all go? Do you think they made it out?"

"They had a better chance at surviving than we did." Grief-stricken, I knew of some who definitely did not make it out in time.

JARVIS

Angelica Orabelle Havens was crying. The three of us were alone. It was dark. *"1, 1, 2, 3, 5, 8, 13, 21 ...*

"Angie, are you all right?" Jared paid a lot of attention to Angelica Orabelle Havens.

"I think so, but I can't feel my foot." Angelica Orabelle Havens was fine.

It was dark. *"34, 55, 89..."* There was a beam of light. *"144 ..."* I pulled them out of the canyon. I pulled them into the cave. My arms and legs hurt. *"233, 377, 610..."* It was dark. It was hard to breathe. *"987; 1,597; 2,584..."* Angelica Orabelle Havens almost killed us. But we didn't die.

ANGIE

I was in a tremendous amount of pain. But we were alive. Jared said we had survived a flash flood followed by a landslide. It felt like the end of the world.

As my eyes adjusted to the dark inside the cave, I began to see why my ankle and foot hurt so much as well as my arms and legs.

"What happened? How did we get here?" I asked Jared as some feeling painfully returned and ripped through my body.

"I had to pull you up onto the first set of rocks," Jared answered apologetically.

"You almost killed him." Jarvis roared. "He could have died because of you!"

"Is that true, Jared?"

"I don't know. You came running up the river by yourself, so I pulled you out. Don't you remember? Then Jarvis came back and helped me pull you up the wall until you started motoring on your own," Jared tried to explain.

"Motoring." Jarvis whispered.

That made me laugh. It was the only normal thing that had happened in the last hour, and it came from one of Jarvis's adorable idiosyncrasies.

Laughing hurt. It hurt in places I did not know could hurt. My ribs were sore, my arm and leg muscles burned, and the pain in my foot was excruciating. I started coughing. Never had I been in so much agony.

Jared scooted over next to me.

"Not doing so good, huh?" His voice was low and soothing.

"No. My foot," I coughed between words, "is it still there?"

"Still there. Let me take a closer look." Jared moved in and bent toward my ankle, this time being extra careful not to touch it.

"Look, but don't touch," I teased.

"What I could use is more light," Jared thought aloud. "Jarvis, do you have that flashlight?"

"Yes."

"How about letting me use it. I promise I won't put my lips on it."

Jarvis had his backpack with him. It was the only pack that made it up the wall and into the cave. Jared's and mine were somewhere at the bottom of the canyon, perhaps in the next state.

Jarvis sneered at Jared's remark, and thankfully relinquished the flashlight without a fight.

"OK, Angie, look away," Jared directed.

"What?"

"Look away. If you want me to check your ankle, you have to look away."

"No. I have a right to know."

Jared shined a small beam of light onto my ankle. I gasped at the sight of my own blood and exposed bone.

"This does not look good. We have to clean it up," Jared asserted.

"No! Don't touch it!"

"Angie, we have no choice. You can't leave it like this, it will get infected."

"It hurts like hell. You'll only make it worse."

"It's going to hurt no matter what we do, but it will hurt more if we don't clean it and try to stabilize it."

The impact had knocked my hiking sandal off. Held tenuously by my crushed ankle, my foot appeared to be dangling from my leg,

"Jarvis, we're going to need the water in your camelback."

"No."

"Jarvis, don't make me come over there and take it from you. You'll regret it."

Jarvis sat still, and Jared impatiently waited.

"The water, Jarvis. Hand it over, now!"

Jarvis took one long sip and then threw the pack over to Jared.

"Thanks."

Jared pulled the camelback bladder out of Jarvis's pack and poured a small amount of water across my ankle. It hurt so bad I thought I was going to pass out. I screamed, and Jarvis screamed along with me. I do not know if it hurt his ears or triggered something else. For his sake and mine, I tried to do a better job absorbing the pain. I stuffed the hem of my T-shirt into my mouth as Jared continued the clean up.

"Jarvis, come over here and hold this light," Jared yelled over our screaming.

"No."

"Jarvis, you have to hold the light. I have to see what I'm doing." Jared was losing patience.

I was losing a battle with consciousness. My shirt muffled my screams. Jarvis held the light, and Jared told me to hang on and be brave. It hurt like hell. I think I passed out. Everything had gone dark, darker than the cave. I heard their voices, but I could not understand or remember what they were saying.

When I opened my eyes again, Jared was sitting beside me shaking his head.

"Jared?" Jarvis asked.

"What?"

"I have my iPhone," he announced sheepishly.

"Jesus, call for help!"

"He's not here, Jared. When are you going to give up that religious crap?"

It was too much. Leave it to Jarvis's cynicism and command of the literal. I was laughing and crying at the same time. My sides were splitting. It felt like my ribs were going to come right through my skin. While imploring Jarvis to call 911, Jared kept working and told me to hold still.

"There's no signal."

"What?"

"There's no signal."

"Let me see that." Jared snatched the phone out of Jarvis's hand. He waved it about wildly. Nothing. Leaving my ankle, Jared crawled about our tomb as he tried to locate a signal. I knew he was not going to find one, but he kept trying and cursing. It was exasperating to watch. We were alone and disconnected from the rest of the world. My body and my mind were crashing.

Not even Jesus was going to save us.

MATHIEU

I was eating dinner alone just as I had done for the past six nights. "World News Tonight" broke into it's own programming with a special report.

"This just in: The National Park Service has confirmed that there has been a flash flood in Zion Canyon late this afternoon. Twenty-one people are known dead, and as many as forty-eight remain unaccounted for. We have just received several amateur videos of the actual event. We want to caution you that some of the footage is graphic."

I watched in horror as water careened along the canyon floor taking rocks, trees, and visitors with it. I squinted and strained my eyes to see if the amateur videographer caught a glimpse of Angelica.

I called Angelica's cell phone as a local news reporter on the scene at the Zion Lodge was introducing a park ranger. I scanned the partially flooded background, searching for anyone who looked like Angelica. Oddly, the sun was shining; however, there was mud, piles of tree limbs, and other debris scattered everywhere. Tall grasses had been mowed down in one direction. It was obvious that something had run through that lower and wider area of the canyon. Everyone there looked official, and they were too occupied to be distracted by the live feed.

She's probably OK. She probably wasn't in the canyon at the time.

I waited to hear her ringback tone, Aerosmith's "Angel." Instead, it went immediately into her voicemail.

There's probably a lot going on. Knowing her, she's probably helping the survivors. I'll call Garrison.

The park ranger was going on about the unpredictability of such phenomena and how storms miles away could have caused the cataclysmic event. The ranger stated that the National Park Service makes it very clear that each person who enters a canyon like Zion does so "at his or her own risk." After the commercial break, Diane Sawyer was going to present a history of flash floods in the surrounding canyons.

Come on, Garrison. Pick. Up.

Voicemail. Shit.

This is not good. Dammit, where are they?

ANGIE

I woke up with Jarvis's shirt wrapped tightly around my leg and ankle, and his backpack was under my head. I was sure that I would once again become his number one enemy for filching his things. The cave was dark. The crack in the rock was barely visible and revealed a shadowy slice of dusk outside.

My eyes were slow to adjust, and I had hoped that I when I was fully awake I would find that everything had been a cruel nightmare. It was so intensely horrific; I was sure it could not have been real. Sadly, with my eyes open, my nightmare continued.

My head was pounding. My mouth was so dry that my tongue stuck to the roof, and my lips adhered to my teeth. My nostrils were encrusted with dust. My arms were sore, and my neck and shoulder muscles screamed when I tried to raise my head from Jarvis's backpack that was cushioning my head from the hard floor of the cave. My left foot felt like it was on fire, yet slowly going numb. I wanted to go home.

"Hey there, are you OK?" Jared's voice was so sweet and full of concern that he made me cry. His tenderness made me all the more homesick. I wanted to be home in my own bed. I wanted my doting mother to fawn over me. I wanted the flowers that I knew Mathieu would send. I wanted to go to the bathroom.

"I just want to go home," I looked up, imploring Jared to take me there.

"I know," Jared said as he brushed his fingers across my forehead and swept my hair out of my eyes. I was able to faintly see his face. Covered with scrapes and grime, he had a very dark and rugged look. Yet his eyes conveyed a caring sympathy.

Jarvis was out of sight, but I could hear his voice.

"There's water dripping back here." Jarvis sounded to be about twenty to thirty feet away.

Jared scooted into a darker part of the cave. He came back and reported that Jarvis was right. A steady stream of water was seeping from the rock ceiling at the back of the cave. If Jared crawled on all fours, he could reach it. After some verbal wrangling, Jared convinced Jarvis to give up his camelback bladder so he could refill it for all to share.

We passed around the replenished vessel. The water was deliciously cool and thirst quenching. The three of us understood the necessity for staying hydrated, so the value of a full camelback bladder was more than priceless; it was sacred.

Water took on a whole new meaning that day. It was like a psychotic governess. It had sent us scurrying up the canyon wall. It wanted to grab us and throw us up against the hard crags and smooth sandstone walls. It sent debris racing down the Virgin River with hopes of snagging us, piercing our flesh, and breaking our bones. It tried to drag us down and drown us. Having failed all that, it became our greatest ally and only hope for life. Without it, we would suffer and eventually perish. What once tried to kill us had become our greatest necessity and our only salvation until we could be rescued.

Jared said that after each drink, he would crawl back and refill the camelback. We could survive without food. Without water we would die within days.

Then there was the delicate matter of urinating and defecating. Exploring the back of the cave with Jarvis's flashlight, the brothers discovered that the water seeping through the rock did not collect inside the cave, so it had to be draining out somewhere below. Peering through the pitch-black void with the small flashlight, they had found a five to six-foot long crevice in the floor. It appeared to be about three feet wide. Fortunately, they discovered it before they fell into it. Jared speculated that if we peed carefully over the back left corner where the rock was relatively flat, it should follow the spring water out. He said he had tried it, and it worked. Easy for a guy to say and do. My plumbing was not designed to work that way and moving in any direction was far too painful for my left foot.

"You have to, Angie. You have no choice." Jared coaxed when I could no longer ignore the intense urge that had built up inside and created intense pressure.

Jared carefully pulled me to the back end of the cave and then to the left. Shining the flashlight on the ceiling to create a soft glow, Jarvis continued counting a little louder to overcome my yelps of torturous pain.

"46,368; 75,025; 121,393..."

Once we reached the area Jared had been talking about, he pulled me around to face the back wall. I fearfully understood what it was he wanted me to do.

"I can't do this," I pleaded. "Let go, you're killing me."

"It will kill you if you try to hold it, and we can't have you stinking up the place."

"Nice, Jared. Besides, you said someone would be here. Where are they?"

Seriousness covered his face as he glared at me from the side. He cocked his head toward Jarvis and mouthed his response.

"I don't know."

Earlier, he had lied to calm Jarvis. He did not know if anyone knew we were missing or where to find us.

"Can you be strong, Angie?" he whispered.

"For Jarvis? Yes."

"For me?"

"I'll try."

Honestly, I did not know if I could be strong for anyone. In the last several hours, Jared had become my strength, and I found myself leaning on him for everything.

"All right, Angie. Let's do this. Think of me as a private nurse. I won't look down. Now, tell me what you need me to do to get you in position above this crevice."

I had to sit on my bare butt and pee over the edge of a rock so urine would not drain back into the cave. I was terribly unbalanced without the use of my left leg, and I had to manage it without getting my feet wet, especially my damaged foot. I was understandably hesitant. My preposterous predicament struck us both as nothing short of comical.

"I can't do this. I'll fall into that chasm, or whatever you want to call it."

"You won't fall. I'll hold you from behind, and I won't let you go."

"What you're asking me to do is too embarrassing."

He moved me closer to the edge of the small chasm between the back wall and us.

"Do you trust me?"

"I don't know."

"I came back and got you, didn't I?"

"Yes."

"I pulled you up the canyon wall, didn't I?"

"No. Jarvis did that," I simpered.

"I managed to wrangle Jarvis's shirt for your ankle, and his backpack for your head, didn't I?"

"Yes."

"I think I've gone above and beyond the call of duty to earn your trust. Would you agree?"

I rubbed my forehead and eyes while contemplating his defense. "OK."

"We have to scoot your butt down just a little farther. You'll have to hold on to my arms, and I'll use my weight to leverage your body. That should keep you from sliding over the edge."

"Are you nuts?"

"It's the only way."

We were in a cramped space. I could not see over the edge.

"How far down is it?"

"I have no idea, maybe five, six feet to the first rock. Don't worry, I won't let you fall."

I was not convinced.

"Do you want me to go first?" Jarvis motioned like he was going to.

"NO! Stop! I'll do it."

I was able to unbutton my shorts. Jared had to help me wrestle them down over my hips and then push them to my bent knees. To get everything out of the way, he gently slid one leg of my shorts off of my good leg and gathered them behind the knee of my damaged left leg. Much to my relief, it was very dark so everything was pretty much concealed. Jared scooted in tight behind me. I could feel the damp fabric of his shorts against my skin. I assumed they had not dried completely from his earlier swim.

"Are you OK with this?" he asked expectantly. He was always the gentleman.

"Yes. Just don't let me go. Are you OK?"

"Yes. This is kind of nice." If one could hear smiles, I could certainly hear and feel his.

"OK then, let's just get this over with."

He placed his hands around the outside of my legs and under my knees. Then he pulled them up slightly.

"Angie, I am going to scoot you to the very edge."

He gently shimmied me out a little farther. I felt the solid rock disappear from under me. It was replaced by a cool breath of air against the tender area now exposed to the dark depths below. If he let go, I would fall. My dangling foot felt like it was going to come unhinged. I clenched my teeth in pain and grabbed ahold of his muscular arms. *They were rock hard, like other parts unknown to me.*

You'll want to lean over as far as you can. I won't drop you."

"Argh! I can't do this! I can't do this with you here." I am sure I sounded whiney. "You're killing me. My foot is killing me! It hurts so bad." I was yelling at him. Poor Jared, he was only trying to help.

"Then get it over with. I'm staying right here. You can't do this without me. Think warm thoughts. Think about peeing in swimming pools." His lips were right at my ear and he spoke softly. "Come on, Angie, you can do this. I'll wait all day if I have to."

"I don't pee in swimming pools," I corrected him.

"Yes, you do. Everybody does."

He was making me laugh, again. It hurt. My knees pressed into my ribs and sent a shooting pain upward of another level.

"Well, in a pool no one knows if I'm peeing. I can't do this with you right here, because you'll know."

"Angie, have you ever seen a stallion or a bull pee in a field? They don't care if anyone is watching." Jared was chuckling.

"You're just trying another stream of logic." I knew his tactic.

"Stream? Did you just say stream?"

"No."

"Yes, you did!"

Oh, it hurt to laugh. Even Jarvis was laughing some distance away. He had overheard the whole conversation. There was nothing humorous about anything going on in that cave. I was in pain, and I had to pee like no tomorrow, which made it all the more hysterical.

So, I just let it go. I could no longer hold it. Urine finally gushed forth. Suspended over a chasm at Jared's mercy, I leaned forward as far as I could, and Jared held tight.

"That's it Angie! Go for it, girl!" cheered Jared, my private nurse and coach. He held on to the backside of my legs to keep them spread apart. Everything stayed dry except the rock below my butt. I screamed in pain while he shouted in victory. Jarvis screamed like a girl, and no one could hear us. We were going to die and rot right there in that hole-in-the-wall, and no one would ever know.

Jared was right; following the path of the spring water, it drained out of the cave. After moving me back, and helping me with my shorts, Jared went back to the crevice. He held both his hands under the spring to collect water and pour it down over the urine soaked rock below.

He crawled back to where I was slouched.

"Now, that wasn't so bad, was it?"

"Where did you learn so much about the workings of the female anatomy?"

Jared paused. "I was married once."

That was a revelation.

"He married Erin Leigh McCann the Whore. You do not know her." Jarvis filled in the blanks.

"I'm sorry."

"It's OK. She was sleeping with my best friend. I didn't see it coming."

"I'm so sorry. How long ago?"

"He has been divorced for 1 year, 1 month, and 21 days or 416 days," Jarvis answered for his older brother. Actually, Jarvis was very forthcoming about his older brother.

"We were only married for 7 years.

"7 years, 2 months, and 18 days, or 2,634 days, to be exact," Jarvis chimed in.

"Well, she made a terrible mistake," I said hoping to add consolation, whether he needed it or not.

"Thanks, you didn't have to say that. The funny thing is, I really miss her. I could never take her back, but I do miss her."

"You did a great job back there, coach. Thanks."

I prayed that we would be rescued before I had to choose between pooping and dying. When it came to our fate, I guessed that I would be the first to die, and I was OK with that because if it happened that way, I would be spared the horror of watching the other two suffer and die trying to save me, again. Plus, I did not want to be left to die alone.

Is it possible that one of them will be left to die alone?

I was flooded with guilt. Had I not turned to join them in Zion, they probably would have made it out. I had messed up and took them with me. Erin Leigh McCann may have been the whore, but I felt like the devil.

MATHIEU

I tried for an eternity to reach Angelica's cell phone. Voicemail.

Garrison's cell phone gave me the same result. So I resorted to doing something I would have never done under normal circumstances. I called Camille.

"Have you heard from Angelica?"

"Angie, you can call her Angie, you know."

There was a lot of background noise. She was either at a bar or a party.

"Where are you?"

"I'm at the University Club. Where are you?"

"Camille, haven't you heard? There's been a flash flood at Zion."

"So?"

"Angelica's there!"

"What?"

"It's all over the news. There's been a flash flood and 21 people are known dead and more are missing. I can't reach Angelica. She's not picking up her cell phone."

"Oh. My. God! She's there?"

"Yes. She went on to Zion. You didn't know?"

"No. Where are you?"

"At home."

"I've got to get out of here. Shit. What'll we do?"

"Stay put. I'll send my driver for you. He'll call you when he reaches the club. It should take him about 15 minutes to get there. You'll come back here."

"Why there? I mean that's OK, but..."

"You and I are the only people who know where she is. We've got to find her and bring her back home."

Dammit, I knew this was not going to end well.

JARED

We were in real trouble. As the other two drifted off to sleep, I kept watch and contemplated our escape and hopeful rescue.

The temperature in the cave was dropping like a stone. I could hear Angie shivering. I had nothing to wrap around her. When the flash flood chased us up the canyon wall, I had no idea that I would need my shirt or my boots. I wondered if anyone had found them downriver.

Jarvis coughed and turned. He had graciously allowed Angie to use his backpack as a pillow. His shirt was wrapped around her ankle. I had to threaten him before he would give it up. He rested his head on his elbow and was still angry with me when he eventually fell asleep.

Jarvis and I had nothing to eat since our snack in the afternoon. I had no idea when Angie last ate. Thank God we had water.

"Jared?" Angie whispered through the darkness.

"I'm right here."

"I'm so cold..."

She was not alone. My fingers and toes were going numb. I was bare-chested and wearing only the wet shorts and boxer briefs that I had on when I climbed out of the river. They were still slightly damp around the waist and pockets. I was limited in what I could do to help either one of us. I looked over toward Jarvis. It was difficult to see anything, but I knew he was not wearing much more. I could hear him breathing, so I could only assume that he was surviving. Angie was the one who was the most vulnerable.

I laid down on the cool rock and slid my body up against her back.

"Are you OK if I try to keep you warm like this?"

"Yes. I'm so cold." She was half asleep, but she had the presence of mind to know where she was and whom she was with. Being careful not to touch her foot with mine, I pressed my body into her back and wrapped my arm around her waist. She took her hand and laced her fingers through mine.

"I'm so sorry, Jared. I feel like this is all my fault," she said in soft tones of deep regret.

"It's not so bad. How often do I get to curl up with a beautiful woman?"

She chuckled. "I could think of better reasons to curl up with someone." Her voice was filled with sarcasm.

"So tell me, how big is your fiancé? Is he going to beat the crap out of me when we get back?"

"He'll have to get through me first."

"Oh, so he's a pipsqueak."

Angie shot her elbow back and into my ribs.

"Ouch! That hurt. I won't be so gentle the next time I have to haul your sweet ass up a mountainside."

"No offense, but I hope there is no next time for my sweet ass, or yours."

Silence. I felt her shiver.

"I'm sorry, too, Angie. I'm sorry I gave you such a difficult time about doing this trip on your own and demanding that you come with us."

"You have nothing to be sorry about. I came back because I wanted to, not because you begged me to."

"Oh, so I begged, did I?"

"Yes. You were pathetic, and I took pity."

She was still shivering. I was, too.

"OK, so let's see what we can do to warm up here. Let's think about a tropical vacation," I suggested. I heard Jarvis cough and shift.

"Is he OK?" Angie asked.

"He's OK. I just checked on him. Now, let's see, where were we?"

"Someplace tropical…"

"Hmm…" Subconsciously I pulled her closer to me.

"Have you ever been to Hawaii?" she asked.

"No, have you?"

"Yes. It' beautiful! The warm winds tickle your skin and the sun-soaked beaches warm your back. You can rent private secluded cabins that open up to the water and no one can see what you're doing. Or, you can charter a bareboat yacht and sail the islands nude."

"You've sailed in the nude?" The vision was exquisite.

"Well, it was just me and …"

She silenced.

"Angie?"

"Nothing. I think you would like it, Jared."

"I think I would too, with the right person."

"Definitely, with the right person…"

Silence.

"I don't think this is helping. It's like being on a diet while obsessing about your favorite dessert. It just makes me crave what I can't have." She had adequately summed up our brief attempt to conjure up warmth.

Silence.

As another shudder rolled through her body, I felt her grab my arm a little tighter and squeeze my fingers a little harder. I moved in closer. Fuck the chivalry. Fuck her damn fiancé. She was not going to freeze to death on my watch. I moved my hips into her and spooned tightly up against her back. Was it arousing? Of course it was. I would dare any warm-blooded man to be that close to a beautiful woman like Angie and not react. If it generated heat in my body, then let it be, and let it transfer to her. It was all for the good.

Jarvis coughed fitfully and drew his knees as close to his chest as he possibly could. The increased severity of his spasmodic hacking frightened Angie.

"Should he be over here with us?"

"I doubt he'll come over."

"Make sure he knows that he's invited," Angie directed.

"I don't know if that's such a good idea, but let me try." Angie may have been clueless about Jarvis's reaction to being touched. On the other hand, my resistance to inviting him could have been easily misinterpreted. I had no choice but to risk it.

"Jarvis." No response. "JARVIS," I spoke louder. Though no one was nearby to hear, I still had this odd aversion to rudely shout at him, so I excused myself and crawled over to his side of the cave where he was curled up in a tight fetal position.

I shook him. His skin was cold. "JARVIS, wake up!" He jolted at the touch of my hand. His fist came at me and connected with my jaw. He followed through with his body and landed on top of me. Angie screamed when she heard the scuffle. I tried to reason with him.

"JARVIS! JARVIS! Wake up! It's me!"

He sat on my chest and started pummeling my face. I straight armed his shoulder and kicked him to the other side. He landed precariously close to Angie who was now shouting at us to stop. Jarvis came back at me. I had no choice. I gave him a shot to his gut with my right foot.

"Ugh!" He rolled off and back to his corner.

"Son of a bitch! Don't ever touch me again, asshole." Jarvis was doubled over, cursing a blue streak.

"Jarvis! I was just trying to see if you wanted to keep warm with us.

"NO! Pervert." He slid back into his corner of the cave and huddled up against the rocks. "Leave me alone, moron."

The cave silenced. I sat shivering between a brother who was repelled by me and a woman that I was inappropriately attracted to.

Angie drifted back to sleep. As she shook and whimpered, I prayed for the three of us. I prayed for my mom. I imagined she would die a thousand deaths when she realized that Jarvis and I were in the canyon during the flash flood. Nine hundred and ninety-nine of them would be for Jarvis. I prayed for Angie's parents and I prayed for Mathieu. If I were him, I would have died a thousand deaths if I knew she was missing.

CAMILLE

Just as Mathieu had said, Donald pulled up in front of the club approximately 15 minutes after I hung up. My flashy exit, escorted by Mathieu Dufour, did not turn out the way I had hoped. Donald marched in, grabbed my arm, pulled me away from the bar, and marched me back out to Mathieu's over the top black Lincoln Navigator. I felt more like an errant child than a celebrity.

In the back seat of the Navigator, I tried several more times to call Angie. No response. I checked her Facebook page and Twitter account to see if she had posted any messages since the reported flash flood. Nothing. I was not surprised. She had only called twice since her departure for the airport a week ago.

The ornate iron gates opened as the Navigator approached the long drive leading up to Mathieu's estate home. Donald had not spoken a single word to me. Either he was really mad, or he was under orders to stay quiet.

Leaning on one of the large white columns of the portico, Mathieu was impatiently waiting outside for us. When the Navigator pulled in front, Mathieu hurriedly approached the SUV and opened the door for me.

"Come, Camille. We've got to work fast."

Mathieu was not wasting any time. Apparently, a pleasant "how are you?" would have cost too much. I followed him inside to a large office just to the left of his entrance hall.

"Would you like something to drink?" He did not bother to wait for my response. "No, I see that you're already well hydrated. Have a seat." He waved to a large wingback chair as he walked around to the front of his desk, leaned back on it, and stared down at me.

"We allowed this to happen, you and me," He stated accusingly.

"What? What are you talking about? There's no way we could have stopped any of this."

"No. But when her parents hear about it they will want to know why we didn't stop her. They will want to know why we didn't tell them what Angelica was up to."

"Because she specifically asked us not to speak a word of it to them. She was direct about wanting us to cover for her. And why are we here arguing this? We should be putting our energies toward getting out there and finding her." I was absolutely dumbfounded by his priorities. "What are you scared of, anyway?"

His smartphone rang.

"Simon, what do you have? ... I see. .... Of course we need to find him, too. Find Angelica and you will find Garrison. ... Yes, of course we want to find the young men... Yes."

Listening intently to the voice on the phone, Mathieu stood up from his desk and began to pace around his spacious office.

"OK, but hear me loud and clear. You focus on finding Angelica and bring her back safe and sound first. How soon are you leaving? ... Good. I'll speak to Aidan about getting the drone out as soon as he can. Good luck and bring her back."

He disconnected his call and walked back to me.

"You need to tell her parents. I'll handle mine."

"Why me? She wasn't running from me."

Mathieu stared at me with his entrancing dark blue eyes that have captured many a young girl's heart, I was sure of it.

"Because I've got to take care of my parents. They are understandably irate. We need to make sure every effort is being made to find Angelica and the man I sent to track her." Agonized, he rubbed his forehead. His cell came alive again.

"Dad. What's up?"

I could not make out what was being said, but if the tone of voice escaping his cell phone was any indication, Mathieu's dad was ripping him a new one. It went on for some time. I was very uncomfortable witnessing the berating that he was receiving.

"Say what you want, Dad. If I had not sent Garrison to follow her, we would not have known that Angelica was in Zion."

The voice on the other end went ballistic. I excused myself. Mathieu snapped his fingers at me and pointed to the chair, as in "Sit your ass back down."

"Yes. I know he was our number one man. Why the hell do you think I sent him?"

Mathieu's voice suddenly softened.

"Where did they find him? ... I'm so sorry... That's awful. ... Yes, I will contact the search team."

Mathieu circled behind his desk and quickly jotted down a number. His dad must have calmed down as well. The audible yelling had stopped.

"Yes, Dad. Of course I'll talk to her parents. ... Yes. I'll let them know that we will do whatever it takes to find her. ... No, I don't know why. ... Thanks, Dad."

The sexy man who was leaning on his desk earlier was hunched over and reeling from the news. The corporation's number one security agent's lifeless body was found drowned near the Temple of Sinawava. It was unknown how far it had traveled.

"Mathieu," I stood and gently placed my hand on his arm. "I'm sorry. I didn't know you were having her followed. I'm sorry about your agent. I'll give Angie's parents a call. I can take care of that. There's a good chance they already know."

CHAPTER ELEVEN

ANGIE

The next morning I woke up in agony. The truth was, I did not sleep much at all. I was terribly cold and in excruciating pain. When I was not in pain, which was never, I kept waking up because I was nervous about other possible invisible inhabitants of the cave like spiders, snakes, or bats. When I turned to try and find a more comfortable position, I would discover another limb or body part that had been drug over the rocks. My arms were bruised and felt like they had been yanked out of their sockets from the guys' strong grips. Jared and Jarvis spared me no mercy during their rescue efforts. I was deeply grateful.

Sometime during the night, Jared had slipped in against my back trying to help us produce and preserve whatever warmth our bodies could generate. He invited Jarvis to join us, but that did not turn out so well. After a scary scuffle, Jarvis retreated and retrenched farther away from us. Jared eventually rejoined me. I felt better when he was near.

I woke up for short spurts throughout the night. My mind naturally wandered to things that made me feel safe. First, I thought about my parents. Had they heard about the flash flood or the landslide? Were they on their way to Utah to find me? How was my mother holding up? Were they blaming themselves? Or, were they really pissed that I left without telling them where I was going? Was my mother crying? I could not begin to imagine how my father would handle the news. I had never seen him in a panic. He was usually so calm, even in the most stressful situations.

I was truly sorry, too. Sorry for the worry my parents may have been experiencing. Sorry that Jared and Jarvis had to come back and rescue me. Sorry I was stuck in a cave. Sorry about the one-sided fistfight that broke out because of my suggestion. Back home, I suspected Mathieu would blame himself for my disappearance, and he did not deserve that. I was sorry for everything. I felt like the most pitiful and selfish person on the face of the earth.

Jarvis stirred first. He moaned as he stretched and asked where he was. Squinting in the dim light of the dark cave, he looked over at me, and then his face dropped. He remembered.

"Where's Jared?" His voice was monotone, leaving no emotional hooks for me to latch on to.

"He's right here on the other side of me keeping warm." I responded with my fingers to my lips, hoping Jarvis would get the signal to keep his voice down, if he could see us at all.

"My arms and legs hurt," Jarvis understandably complained, "and I'm hungry. Can I have my backpack back, please?" Jarvis had lent me his backpack to use as a pillow.

I pushed it toward him as far as I could reach without losing Jared's arm hold around my waist.

Jarvis pulled it beside his still partially reclined body, put the tube of the camelback bladder to his lips, and took a long draw of water. My mouth was scorched. I was extremely thirsty, and my throat was stinging from an escalating blaze that was rising up from my esophagus. As I watched Jarvis, I tried to imagine the feel of cool clear liquid trailing down my throat and putting out the fire that seemed to be burning out of control from the back of my tongue to the pit of my empty stomach.

Then Jarvis did the most unexpected thing. He sat up, pulled his pack into his lap, proceeded to unzip one of the outside compartments, and pulled out a granola bar. He looked like a raccoon that just hit the jackpot. Right on cue, my stomach growled loudly. It was filled with nothing but morning acid. As Jarvis began ripping the wrapper from the bar, Jared stirred beside me. He put his hand to his forehead and raked his hair from his eyes.

"Hey, Angie, how are you feeling?" he whispered. My name seemed to roll from his lips like a pleasant dream. I turned to answer. The blows he received from Jarvis the night before had transformed his face overnight. I gasped.

"Oh my gosh! You look like hell."

"I'll have to take your word for it. Though I feel like I was run over by a semi. What happened? Was I out of line last night? Did I do something inappropriate?"

Jarvis's antennae went up. He did not jump in. He just sat up a little higher and continued to eat his granola bar. The paper around the bar crumpled again and caught Jared's attention.

"Where did you get that?" Jared questioned his brother suspiciously.

"My backpack."

"Do you have any more?"

Jarvis pulled his pack back into his lap, tore the zipper back, and rummaged again. After several seconds he lifted his head.

"Nope, that was the last one. What happened to your face?"

Jared went to lunge at him. I grabbed his arm, wrenching my leg in the process.

JARED

Even though we were sequestered from direct sunlight, heat was building inside the cave, and according to Jarvis's watch, it was only 10:30 in the morning. I never used the word "buried" around Angie and Jarvis. It sounded too final. I think I said we were temporarily trapped by a large amount of rock and dirt that covered the opening, and it was time to do something about it.

Jarvis and I began inspecting and pulling at the debris that blocked the small entrance. Our muscles were aching from pulling Angie out of the canyon the day before. We dug earnestly, groaning and moaning as we worked. We scraped at the dirt with our hands until we loosened the first rock and were able to push it out of the way. We listened to it tumble down the canyon wall and land with a faint splash in the water below. It sounded far below, farther than I remembered climbing up. *Was it possible that yesterday's violence carved out the canyon floor making it deeper? Or, did we really climb that high?*

With each rock or large amount of sediment that we moved away, more daylight filtered into the cave, and it became apparent that we were perched high in the air. I tried squeezing my head through the opening to get a better view of our surroundings. I was unsuccessful. We needed to dig more. Our fingers were raw, our knuckles were scraped and bleeding, and our fingernails were filled with dirt. Our arms, backs, and legs were screaming. The dust we were stirring up clung to our sweat drenched bodies making our task very uncomfortable.

As we scratched, clawed, and shoved, we heard a low hum and the sound of rotors.

"A Helicopter! It's a helicopter! They're coming! They're coming to get us!" Jarvis was right. Slowly scouring the path of the Virgin River from above, a helicopter was headed our way.

Angie sat up. Her eyes were wide open, and her mouth broke into a smile reviving the dimples I had missed so much. She tried to pull her body across the floor of the cave to see for herself. The helicopter crept deliberately up the river. It was low enough that as it passed overhead, the vibration of its rotors could be felt in our chests and shook the ceiling and walls of our prison. Angelica screamed for help. Waving our arms and shouting, Jarvis and I leaned out as far as we could.

"I can't see it. I can hear it, but I can't see it," I called out. "Dammit, they're going to miss us. They can't see us! Dig, dammit, dig!"

Jarvis and I began raking our raw fingers across the rock and dirt. We tried battering the walled opening with our shoulders. The sound of the helicopter grew fainter, and just as gradually as it had approached, it eventually faded and became inaudible.

I leaned back against a sidewall, pulled my knees up, and dropped my head into my hands.

"They can't see us. The canyon's too narrow for them to fly down through it. The ledge above is acting as a canopy, and we haven't cleared enough away. SHIT!

Angie was holding on to her ribs. She was in more pain than she was letting on. Her foot, which she dragged across the cave, was black and blue. It dangled like an overripe piece of fruit. Her ankle had to be broken or, worse yet, shattered.

"OK, which one of you rocks is responsible for this?" I shouted referring to everything around us.

I gave the one closest to my corner a strong kick with my foot, and to my surprise, I met it with no resistance. I nearly hurled myself out with it. Several other boulders near the center gave way and careened down the canyon wall behind it. That one act of rage cleared a large opening. Not only could I stick out my head, but my entire body.

Jarvis and I jumped back as we heard something shake loose above us. The last rock must have been a support for a larger section. We fell farther back as the sky began to fall. The cave quickly filled with a plume of choking dust. I scurried back next to Angie and tried to cover her. The cave floor vibrated violently. The sound of our screams, gags, and sputters assured me that we were still together. Gasping for air, the heaving of Angie's chest was wrenching her body and made it impossible for her to stay immobile. The thrusts were sending jolts of pain down her leg and through her foot. I could tell she was in agony as she tried to regain control. Hoping to at least immobilize the lower half of her body as she desperately fought for oxygen, I reached over her and grabbed her hips.

I was gagging badly, but managed to yell through it.

"Put you hands over your mouth, or breathe through your shirt."

Through the dim light, thickened by dust molecules hanging in the air around us, I could see her raise her arm to her mouth. Jarvis did the same. An answered prayer later, the sliding earth seemed to stop. Only the last pebbles could be heard rolling past the opening. One last rock hit the river below. Hanging like a veil between us, the dust inside our sandstone capsule started to thin. Fortunately, the opening we had carved out remained open.

"Jarvis, are you OK?" I could no longer hear him choking. "JARVIS!"

"196,418; 317,811; 514,229..."

Angie continued breathing through her shirt. The scare was exhausting. I performed one last hack of my throat to clear my airway. Angie's head wavered and her eyes rolled, so I quickly scooted in behind her to steady her limp body and keep her from slumping over.

"Jarvis, bring me the water." I called out to my ciphering brother.

He did not move. He was listening. I listened, too. That was when I heard what he was listening to. Nothing. It confirmed my worst fear. The water running through the ceiling at the back of the cave had stopped.

Jarvis crawled over with his camelback.

"Go check," I directed as I took the camelback from him and held the mouthpiece up to Angie's lips. I did not have to tell Jarvis what to check. He knew.

When I was convinced that Angie was stabilized and breathing normally, I crawled to the front ledge of the cave to examine the opening we had punched out. It was worse than I first thought. There was a steep drop below us, and a small ledge that jutted out above us. The mouth that saved us was now preventing our rescue with its overbite. It concealed us from anything that could walk or fly overhead. It appeared we were positioned 30-50 feet below what I believed to be the rim. Because the overhead ledge of rock blocked our visibility, it was hard to tell exactly how far we were from the top. The wall on the opposite side was a mere twenty to thirty yards away. It was like being trapped in an elevator shaft with no roof.

I slid back into the cave. Jarvis was full of questions.

"Where's Mom?"

"I don't know."

"Where's Mom?"

"I told you, I don't know. Probably on her way to the Lodge." I made it up. For all I knew, the Lodge could have been wiped out with the torrents of water that went through and managed to carve out the riverbed below us. It took a lot of water to do that much damage. I could only imagine what had happened downstream.

"When will we get out of here?"

"I don't know. Soon."

"How soon?"

"Maybe in a couple of hours."

I estimated we were approximately three miles from the Temple of Sinawava when the flashflood hit. We did not have the required permits to go farther up river, so someone had to know, within three to four miles, where we were located. That was assuming someone saw us, and they had survived.

Someone had to know. They sent a helicopter, didn't they?

We remained silent for a time, hoping to hear the chopper return. It did not. It must have taken a different route back.

"I'm thirsty," Jarvis whispered.

I handed the camelback back to him. "Drink sparingly."

"Why?"

"In case it takes them a little longer to find us."

"You said they would find us today."

"Probably."

"Which is it, Jared? Will it be today? Tomorrow? When?"

There was no satisfying Jarvis. There were no definitive predictions that I could give him. There were no black and white anchors to hold on to.

JARVIS

We were stuck in a cave with Angelica Orabelle Havens. She was hurt, and Jared liked her. He helped her pee on a rock and drink water from my bladder. *Ha ha!* Jared said to stop calling it that and start calling it a camelback. He said he did not want to play games.

Jared was no fun anymore. He was too worried about Angelica Orabelle Havens. A boulder fell on her foot and smashed it. It looked gross. Jared slept with her. Well, not like that. He slept next to her to keep her warm. Not *with* her. Jared would never do that. They were not married. Angelica Orabelle Havens was engaged to Mathieu Olivier Dufour. I do not know Mathieu Olivier Dufour, but I know that he is a fucking idiot. (I am not allowed to say that word.) I think she should dump Mathieu Olivier Dufour, but Jared said I had to stop saying that, too. Jared made a lot of extra rules on our trip about what I could and could not say. Jared was no fun anymore.

The second day in the cave, we heard a helicopter. It was looking for us. Jared said they had to be looking for *us* because we heard no other screams.

Jared got angry, and he created a landslide. He pushed a big boulder, and all of the rocks above slid down the side of the canyon. We could hear them splashing into the water. Jared said he almost fell out of the cave, but I caught him, so he did not.

Jared and I looked outside and guess what? We were hanging in mid-air. There was no trail up or down. We were stuck. But Jared said they would find us. He took my empty backpack and hung it over the edge like a flag. Jared said it would help them find us. Oh, and the really bad news: the water stopped dripping in the back of the cave.

I think Jared liked Angelica Orabelle Havens the way some people like sick animals or babies. I told Jared she would get better. He was very worried. He made her drink water. He sat with her and told her funny stories. When he ran out of stories, I told her about Jared's football games. She liked that. I told her Mathieu Olivier Dufour was a fucking idiot. I forgot. Not really. Jared made me go away.

I had a place in the cave that Jared said belonged to me. He gave me a sharp stone so I could write my numbers on the rock wall. He said not to write too big and to leave plenty of space. He promised me that he and Angelica Orabelle Havens would not come and bug me in my space. My head faced north when I slept there. I made sure. I could watch the sun cross over the canyon at noon, too.

"832,040; 1,346,269; 2,178,309..." It takes more time when you have to scratch the numbers into the rock. I was going to be Michelangelo Fibonacci Gauss the Fucking Caveman.

"Oops!"

JARED

"LISTEN! It's another helicopter! They're coming back! They must know we're here!

Angie popped up on her elbows. Life seemed to spring back into her weakened body. Jarvis and I rushed to the opening of the cave and began waving our arms out of the entrance as far as we could without falling over the edge. Perched precariously above the canyon, we stretched out our arms and hands reaching for the sunlight that was just beyond the shadow cast by the rocky overhang. Feeling helpless we began to yell.

Where was my voice?

My throat was so dry, and it hurt to scream.

Where was my voice that could be heard across a football field calling out to Brett for the elusive "Hail Mary?"

Hoping to gain the helicopter's attention, I reached for Jarvis's backpack and began shaking and waving it. We continued screaming even after the sound of the rotors had left us. Once again, all we could hear was the rushing water of the river below. I hated that river. I hated the canyon. I hated everything.

"Did they see you? Are they coming for us?" Angie's hope was sky high. "How will they get us out of here?"

CHAPTER TWELVE

MATHIEU

The death toll had reached forty-six, and twenty-four people remained unaccounted for. Angelica's name was added to the list of the missing. It was reported that she was last seen traveling with the Lawson brothers, Jared and Jarvis.

"Aidan, how soon until we can launch the drone?"

"It should be ready late tonight. I'll give it a test flight in the morning."

"No test flight. As soon as it's ready, we take the corporate jet out to Cedar City Airport. Dad has a helicopter and pilot lined up to take us to the search and rescue site."

"Mathieu, don't get your hopes up. We've never flown the drone in that type of terrain. Remember, we only get to crash her once. Then it's over."

"There will be no crash. See to it."

ANGIE

As soon as the sun dropped below the rim, the temperatures plummeted on what would be our second night in the cave. I had not eaten since breakfast the morning before. Jarvis was quick to point out that I had not eaten in 38 hours. Jared was just as quick to point out that Jarvis *had* something to eat just 14 hours ago while "the rest of us are starving."

When the sun disappeared and our shelter turned dark, the three of us settled in for the night. Jarvis said it was 9:06 PM. Admittedly, our 48-hour deodorants were being put to the test. The day had proven to be very stressful as we tried and failed to attract the attention of two helicopters. Not to mention, Jared and Jarvis had performed some heavy-duty excavation.

When Jarvis finally stopped his scribbling on the cave wall and lay down, he quickly fell asleep. We snickered at the sound of his soft snore. Jared slipped cautiously in behind me. Once more we spooned together for warmth. It was not as cold as the previous night, but I was shaking uncontrollably. Jared rolled onto his back and allowed me to use his shoulder as my pillow.

"How are you doing?"

"I don't know."

He placed his hand on my forehead.

"Jeez, Angie, you're burning up."

Jared slid out from beneath me and retrieved the camelback bladder.

"I need you to drink." He carefully sat me up and held the bladder while I drew in the priceless water.

"Easy. Small sips," he coached.

Wrapping his arms around me, Jared held me close. He was my safe haven, and in the comfort of his strength, I exhaled deeply.

"Talk to me, Angie. Are you going to be OK? Just one more night and they will be here in the morning."

That was the last thing I heard him say before I drifted off to sleep and into my dream world.

Jared was dressed in a white linen shirt and jeans. His bare feet were set comfortably on either side of the horse he was riding bareback. The horse was a chestnut stallion that had a wide white stripe down its muzzle. It shook its head and whinnied as they approached me. On a lead line and prancing steadily behind was a beautiful palomino mare. Jared's eyes lit up brightly when he saw me.

"Come with me," he sang. *"We'll drink and lie under the weeping willow until time finds us there..."*

There was a shift, and Jared became Mathieu.

"Come with me, and we'll drink the finest wine and lie under the cottonwood until time finds us there..."

I mounted the mare and took off at a full gallop racing across an open field leaving everything and everyone behind. There was a storm on the horizon, and the sky turned dark as coal. I saw a barn in the distance, but the mare had left me. I remained to walk the tree-lined lane alone. Due to the accelerating wind, the trees began to sway, and yellow maple leaves blew across my path like weightless gold coins. As I approached the farmhouse, I heard the shutters bang against the white clapboard siding. A loose screen door slapped haphazardly with each heavy gust. It appeared that no one was home, so I scaled the steps leading up to the deteriorating wraparound porch.

I was standing in the middle of the large farmhouse. It was cold and empty. Turning to the right, I entered what I guessed to be the parlor. Its heavy drapes were pulled close. Peering through the dim space, I saw that it was furnished in fine antiques and leather, but it felt empty and sad. I was hopelessly alone. Moving down the center hall, I crossed into the kitchen. Set out on an overworked butcher's block, the crackers were stale, and the cheese had turned a putrid black and blue with mold. There was nothing safe to eat. The room laughed and ridiculed my hunger.

Mathieu casually strolled through the doorway. He was expecting me. Wearing his charming one-sided grin, he approached and seductively offered me a glass of wine. He made a toast in my honor. The wine was much too sweet for my liking. Mathieu thought it was superb. He wrapped his arms around my waist and kissed me softly. His sweetened tongue swirled in my mouth and wet my lips. Happy to be in his potent embrace, I forgot my surroundings. I was aroused, and I wanted him. His hand moved across my buttocks while his other hand cupped my face. I returned his beckoning and began pulling at his belt buckle.

Wait... the lips were Jared's, and Jared's hands were caressing me, and Jared's eyes were taking me. I felt him move and surge. He was rough and aggressive. I reached and took hold...

I rolled over and struck my foot.
"Ouuuuuuwa! Arrrrgghh! I felt lightning roll through my left leg. I was shaking.
"Shhh, shhh. I'm right here." It was Jared. "Drink this." He placed the water to my lips. "Slowly, that's it."
I closed my eyes and laid my head back on his chest. I heard him softly reassure me. I thought I heard him praying.

JARED

By the third day, I feared Angie was in real danger. *Where was everyone? Where are the helicopters? Why has no one come back? What did they report to our parents? Dear God, what if my mother thinks we're dead? What if they're not coming back? What if they've called off the search?*
We had not eaten in days. We were virtually out of water. I had given the last of the camelback to Angie. She had struggled in her parched state to suck out the last drop. Jarvis had become hysterical during the night. He was demanding answers. He would not leave the edge of the cave opening, hoping upon hope that the helicopters were coming back. I ineffectively tried to coax him back in. I was torn between staying with Angie and keeping her warm, and keeping Jarvis safe from falling asleep and rolling over the edge.
After checking on Jarvis one last time, I crawled back into the cave next to Angie and kept my eyes on Jarvis's silhouette provided by a kind moon. I prayed as my mother had taught me.

"Our Father, who art in heaven, hallowed be Thy name. Thy Kingdom come, Thy will be done on earth as it is in heaven. Give us this day our daily bread, and forgive us our trespasses, as we forgive those who trespass against us. And lead us not into temptation, but deliver us from evil for Thine is the Kingdom, and the power, and the glory forever.

God Bless Mom, Jarvis, and Angie. Dear God, please keep Jarvis safe while he watches and waits in his sleep. I know he doesn't believe in You, but I also know You love him just the same, maybe more. Yeah, way more.

Please save Angie. Relieve her pain and keep her safe from infection. Don't let her suffer. It feels like I am losing her. Please, God, don't take her away from me. And bring us water. We need water. We need food. We need to be rescued. Please save us from this hell... And God, I pray that that family made it back to safety. I pray that by some miracle those children are safe at home in their beds. Please hear my prayer. No one else can see or hear us, but I know You can. Please get us out of here alive. And God, bless everyone else in the world. Amen."

JARVIS

I heard Jared praying.

Save your breath, Jared. If there were a God, like you think there is, we would be out of here, and those people would not have died.

CHAPTER THIRTEEN

JARED

The following morning I knew what I had to do. We were out of water. We had had nothing substantial to eat in three days. I had lost weight. My shorts were falling off, and quite frankly, we all smelled bad. The cave smelled bad. Death was making its foul imprint known to us. It hovered like a scavenger. Angie was in bad shape. She was running a fever, and I knew she was dehydrated. She was in and out of sleep all morning.

Jarvis had just about filled the cave wall with his silly numbers. Who knew where they began and ended? It was the only thing that kept him sane. The last time I scooted to the edge to pee, I noticed that he had sketched the constellations above his head. He was whispering more to himself. It could have been because I was spending most of my time consoling and comforting Angie. She managed to stay with me minutes at a time

We were going to die.

"Jarvis, I'm calling a family meeting."

"Ha!" he laughed.

"Let's meet at the edge of the cave."

I crawled to him, and there we sat like two peas in a pod with our feet dangling over the edge and swinging in the air. It felt good to do something so childlike with my brother.

"Jared, we're going to die, aren't we? They're not coming, are they?"

"I didn't mean to lie, Jarvis. I just didn't know."

"I know." And then he rested his head on my shoulder. My brother, my beautiful baby brother, showed me unsolicited affection. Yes, we were going to die. It was so tangible that even Jarvis was willing to speculate. Not wanting to startle him a hundred feet in the air, I carefully placed my arm around his shoulder. He was just too tired to fight me off. We sat quietly together. I held back tears. I thought of our mother, and how she would have cherished our moment.

In a rare occurrence, Jarvis initiated further discussion and broke our silence.

"Jared, let's not die today."

"Oh? Why not today?"

"I think I'll be able to see Cassiopeia tonight."

"Really?"

"Yep."

I had no idea if he knew what he was talking about. It struck me funny that he should think to postpone death for the sake of a constellation. But, hey…

I gathered up his empty camelback - OK, bladder. He loved that word. It was time for me to go. I left Jarvis with strict instructions.

"Listen, Jarvis. I am going to go find water and hopefully something for us to eat. You are going to help me by hoisting me up to that ledge." I pointed to the rock canopy above our heads. "But do not watch. Do you hear me?

"Do. Not. Watch. Me.

"If I fall, do not look down. Promise? Do not look. Do you promise? If I don't make it, do you promise not to look?"

"I promise."

"Don't ever look down. Got it?"

"Got it."

"Don't ever let Angie look down."

"I GOT IT!"

"SHHHHHHH. You'll wake her up. Now, if I get out, but don't make it back tonight, you have to do one important thing for me; you have to keep Angie warm."

"What?"

"You have to keep her warm. She's sick. She's very sick. She's running a fever. She shivers all night. You have to keep her alive. Say you'll keep her warm at night."

"What?"

"Jarvis, what are you going to do at night?"

"Keep Angelica Orabelle Havens warm."

"Yes. Just pretend she's me, but put *her* head on *your* shoulder."

"Angelica Orabelle Havens should dump Mathieu Olivier Dufour."

"Yes, she should. Now, promise."

"OK, Jared. I promise."

"And, say your prayers."

"No. Now you're just being ridiculous."

JARVIS

I pushed Jared up onto the rock. He hurt my shoulder. He almost pushed me over the edge. Angelica Orabelle Havens screamed. We thought she was asleep.

"*3,524,578* ... Jared's feet left my shoulder. He was dangling in the air. Angelica Orabelle Havens was yelling at Jared something about love and shit like that. *5,702,887* ..."

Jared grunted loudly and pulled himself up. I could not see his feet after that; they disappeared somewhere above my head. I could hear him groaning and grunting again. Rubble fell down across the cave opening and hit me in the face. Angelica Orabelle Havens was crying.

After the rubble stopped, I heard Jared.

"Jarvis, I'm Ok. I made it! I'll be back. Hear me?" Then he shouted louder. "Angelica, I'll be back. Jarvis knows what to do. I love you. I love both of you."

Angelica Orabelle Havens closed her eyes. She whispered Jared's name. Her crying finally stopped, and she fell asleep.

"OK, Jared. I promise."

Jared left. I waited. 9,227,465.

Jared went for water. I waited. 14,930,352.

Jared went for food. I waited. 24,157,817.

Maybe Jared would find Mom. I waited. 39,088,169.

Maybe he would find the helicopters. I waited. 63,245,986.

Maybe he would find a stream. I waited. 102,334,155.

Maybe he would find something to eat. I waited. 165,580,141.

~

The sky turned dark, and it was filled with stars. There she was: Cassiopeia. *Could Jared see her, too?*

Jared was not coming back. He left me. He left me with Angelica Orabelle Havens. She did not wake up. She was shaking.

"OK, Jared. I promise."

"Our Father, who art in heaven, hallowed be Thy name. Thy Kingdom come, Thy will be done on earth as it is in heaven. Give us this day our daily bread, and forgive us our trespasses, as we forgive those who trespass against us. And lead us not into temptation, but deliver us from evil for Thine is the Kingdom, and the power, and the glory forever.

God Bless Mom, Jared, ... and Angelica Orabelle Havens, ... and everybody else in the world. ... Amen... Pfft."

I crawled over and sat next to Angelica Orabelle Havens. She smelled bad. Her foot was gross. She was shaking. I touched her. She was breathing. She was still alive. I lay down next to her. I did not move her head.

I was so hungry and thirsty. I had bad dreams.

Jared was eating a cheeseburger and French fries, and he would not share them. Then he showed me his super-sized Coke, and he would not give me a sip. Jared was laughing at me. Then my mom came over and ignored me. She could not see me. She patted Jared on the head, stole one of his French fries, and popped it into her mouth. "Such a good boy," she said. I could not really see her face, but I knew it was Mom. She did not see me. She did not look at me. Why was no one looking for me?

"Jarvis, Jarvis..."

Jared was teasing me. He was holding out a French fry.

"Jarvis! Get up! Get over here and help me!"

What?

"Jarvis? Where are you? Get over here!"

It was Jared. It really was Jared! It hurt to move.

"Jarvis, I have water. Get over here. Can you hear me? JARVIS! ANSWER ME!"

"I'm coming." I crawled over to the ledge. "Jared, is that you?"

I could hear him laugh. It was Jared.

"Who do you think it is? St. Peter?" he asked me.

"Jared..."

"Jarvis, let me see your hand."

I shoved my hand out. God, my arm hurt. (Not the real God. Well, you know what I mean.) My arm looked skinny. Jared lowered the camelback bladder.

"THE BLADDER!" I took it out of the air and pulled it into the cave. I flipped back the clip and sucked on the mouthpiece. It gagged me. Jared heard me.

"Slowly! Suck it slowly!"

The water hurt as it ran down my burning throat. I took several sips, breathed, and then took several more.

"Save some for Angie. Take it back to Angie and give her some. Is she all right? How is she?"

I crawled back to Angelica Orabelle Havens. "I have water. Wake up. Wake up, Angelica Orabelle Havens."

"Is she breathing?" I heard Jared ask.

I put my hand over her nose.

"Yes."

"Thank God. Jarvis, listen to me. Can you get her to sit up?"

"Sit up..."

"Can you do it, Jarvis?"

"Sit up, Angelica Orabelle Havens." I pulled her shoulders. She did not smell good. I did not smell good. The cave did not smell good. There were flies on her ankle.

"Gross."

Angelica Orabelle Havens opened her eyes. I showed her the water.

"He's back?"

"Yes. Jared is outside the cave."

"Jarvis, is she sitting up?"

"Yes."

"Offer her the water."

I held up the tube. She grabbed the mouthpiece and sucked on the tube. She spit up. She tried again.

"Slower!" I yelled at her.

Jared did not come back into the cave. He was afraid. He said it was too dangerous. Jared lowered his shorts. The pockets were filled with blackberries.

"Ha! Ha! Jared dropped his pants!"

Jared did not tell me to shut up that time.

JARED

I never went back into the cave again. It was too risky to climb back down. I was too exhausted and lightheaded. I had covered a lot of miles barefoot and half delirious before I finally found water. I built little piles of stones along the way to make sure I could find my way back to the cave. If I had to go for water again, I should be able to reach the source sooner because the stone markers would guide me directly back.

I lay down and talked to the other two while they ate the berries I was able to gather. It was good to hear Angie's

voice. Because she went all day without water, she
sounded raspier, and she had to exert more effort to speak.
Plus, she had to speak up for me to hear her across the
distance that now separated us.

At her insistence, Jarvis drug her out to the ledge.
She couldn't see me, but she demanded that she be closer.

"Can you stretch out your arm so I can see your
hand?" I asked her.

Through the dark of night and courtesy of the moon,
I could see her fingers reach out beyond the rock. The band
of her engagement ring reminded me that there was
someone out there that was missing her more, if that was
possible. Then Jarvis stuck his arm out so I could see his
hand, too. It dwarfed Angie's, and the two hands
suspended over the canyon together was a warm and
welcomed sight.

"What's it like up there?" Angie asked, as they
withdrew their arms.

"It's beautiful out here, Angie. You can see for miles
during the day. And Jarvis, the stars are magnificent.
Andromeda is spiraling around my head. It's amazing!
There has to be a God, Jarvis."

I heard Jarvis snort. I could tell from the scratching
of rock on rock that he had taken up his stone and began
carving into the ceiling again. *Tomorrow, if we're still here,
I'll try to find him a sharper stone.*

"Jared, did you see anyone else?" Angie asked
hesitantly.

"No. But I saw the weirdest thing before I found
water. I must have been really dehydrated because it was
pretty damn freaky. It could have been a hallucination. But
I'm pretty sure it was real."

"What happened?"

"I was sitting on the edge of a ravine. I could
actually see where the River Walk trailhead used to be. You
know, at the Temple of Sinawava?"

"Used to be?"

"Yeah, the facilities were wiped out. I'm pretty sure
that's where it was. It was a wide opening in the canyon

floor, and there was mud and debris everywhere. It looked like a war zone. Some small parts of the walls were still standing, and in some places the foundations were exposed. There were a few vehicles that looked like they'd been tossed about before landing in a heap. They were all banged up and covered in mud and silt."

"Did you see anybody? Did anybody see you?"

"No, just a herd of mule deer grazing like nothing had happened. I was too far away for them to care about what I was doing there. Anyway, I was looking for a way down. I was pretty sure if I could get down to the canyon floor, I could find my way back to Zion Lodge and hopefully find help there."

"Jared, you have to be careful. I'm sure they're looking for us. Don't put yourself at risk."

"Too late for that! But don't worry, I'll be careful."

"So what happened that freaked you out?"

"Well, I heard this humming. It sounded like a swarm of bees. Have you ever heard a swarm of bees on the move?"

"Yes." It was the first thing Jarvis had said during the entire conversation. Either he was enwrapped or bored to tears.

"I know *you've* seen it. I was with you," I reminded him. "Remember? We ran like hell and left your model rockets behind."

"Yeah, remember the time we shot one through Old Lady Barner's window? *'Old Lady Barner.'* Boy, she was pissed! Mom said we were so bad that we had to move out of the neighborhood. I did not want to move. So, we did not move."

"She was kidding, Jarvis. We weren't going to move." I could hear Angie snicker in the background. It was a good sign.

"We were bad."

"It was an accident. The rocket fell over and blew out Mrs. Barner's picture window. I paid for the window and replaced your rocket. Mom was kidding."

Jarvis thought that was funny. He loved that story.

"So what about the humming?" Angie brought us back. I could imagine her lying on the hard floor of the cave, eyes closed, cold, and uncomfortable. With Jarvis carving his sequences into the rock again, there was no way he was helping her stay warm or keeping her head up. But she sounded content. It was the happiest I had been all day. Listening to her voice was even better than seeing the expansive views from the rim. I would have climbed back down to see her and let her rest her head on my shoulder if I knew, without a doubt, that we'd be rescued the next morning.

"The humming, Jared, what about the humming? Are you OK up there?" Angie was tired and wanted to get on with my revelation.

"Yes. Just thinking. Anyway, the humming was coming toward me, so I got up on my feet to run."

"Just like the bees!" Jarvis laughed. He always found my dilemmas humorous.

"Yes, just like the bees. As it turned out, it wasn't a swarm of bees; it was just one bee. One big black angry bee and it was coming right at me. It looked like a small helicopter. It had a blinking red light on its forehead, and it hovered in front of me like one of those lumbering wood bees. I tried to swat it, and then it was gone."

I paused and debated whether, or not, I should tell her more of what I thought I saw.

"Angie, it had a name on its side."

"It did?"

"Yes. Its name was 'Angelica.' Can you believe it?"

"Mathieu! It's Mathieu!"

"Mathieu's a bee?" Jarvis screamed and howled. I visualized him holding onto his stomach and rolling over in hilarity while Angie rolled her eyes. But I knew exactly what she was saying, and it was no joke. It meant our rescue was at hand.

"Mathieu and a college intern from the University of Delaware were in the process of building a drone. The plan was to use it to view the vineyards, monitor the condition of the grapes, and mostly have a little fun. They were going to apply for their patents, and then sell it."

"That's ingenious…"

"It looks like a small helicopter with a micro-camera on board. It can stream live video. They must know we're here!"

"No. They know *I'm* out *there*."

CHAPTER FOURTEEN

MATHIEU

"He looks like he's in bad shape," Dr. Roberts observed. "He's obviously dehydrated, which isn't surprising. See how his lips are swollen and cracked? His eyes appear sunken, too." Dr. Roberts watched for another thirty seconds. "He seems a little disoriented. He has contusions around his face, arms, and chest. Yeah, he's pretty beat up." Dr. Roberts paused again to study him a little closer. "You said a helicopter's on its way to pick him up?" he asked without taking his eyes off the screen.

"Yes."

"I'll call the hospital and put them on stand-by."

"Doc, I need to talk to him as soon as they bring him in. He can probably tell us where to find Angelica," I pleaded.

The kind doctor put his hand on my shoulder and said, "OK." He recommended that I accompany a search and rescue team member assigned to go down to the hospital to interview Jared Lawson when he arrived.

Because we were able to identify Mr. Lawson, Simon, another security agent who worked for my dad, left the room to call Jared Lawson's next of kin, his mother.

"You said he had a brother that was with him?" the doctor asked.

"Yes. His brother is much younger. We haven't seen him, yet. Either they were separated, or he didn't make it out."

"That's a lot to endure. No wonder he looks so distressed. Let's get him home." The doctor turned and walked away from the monitor.

While the drone, now flying on a low battery, made its way back to base, we sat and waited for the helicopter to pick up Jared. We had failed to locate Angelica, or Jarvis.

Jared's mother had been contacted. Simon described the boys' mother as elated that Jared had been found alive, yet terribly distraught that her youngest son, Jarvis, was not with him. My father immediately chartered a private jet to bring Mrs. Lawson out to Las Vegas. From there, a limo would be waiting to transport her to the University Medical Trauma Center to meet her eldest son.

We raced from the base at Zion Lodge down to Las Vegas to meet Jared Lawson. I had very mixed feelings about Mr. Lawson. On the way, I called Aidan who remained back at base to inspect and recharge the drone.

"How soon can you have it back out? Do you think you can get another flight in before dark?"

"Don't push me, Mathieu. I haven't slept in 36 hours. You coerced me into bringing it out here without a proper test flight. I've never flown it in this type of terrain so I'm flying blind. And, by the way, don't forget we only get to crash it once. You may not agree, but I'm doing my best. We were fortunate enough to find one of them today. Tomorrow, we'll try to find the other two."

"TOMORROW! She could be dead by tomorrow."

Things went from bad to worse. The rescue helicopter sent to pick up Jared could not locate him. Apparently, he had moved from the spot where the drone had found him.

"Dammit. What now? His mother is on the way to Las Vegas expecting to find her son, and we've lost the one person who might know where Angelica is."

We turned around and headed back to base. I had Mrs. Lawson's flight redirected to Cedar City, Utah, where transportation was being arranged to bring her to Springdale.

~

Later that night, I had another discussion with Aidan.

"We have to add audio. We have to be able to communicate with Jared Lawson. We have to tell him to sit tight so we can pick him up."

"Why don't we just tow a sky banner?"

It was a good thing I knew Aidan well enough to know sarcasm was his way of dealing with pressure.

"Mathieu, I don't know that we can add more weight to what we've already got onboard and then fly it at that altitude."

"Make it happen, Aidan. Just make it happen. I'll see you in the morning."

JARED

I had managed to stay awake perched on the rim above the cave that still held Jarvis and Angie as its prisoners. Until they fell asleep, I worked hard to hold a conversation with them. The sound of their voices was soothing to my aching body. Angie was the first to drift off leaving Jarvis and me to contemplate the stars. I tried to find a silver lining to all that had happened.

"We never see stars like this at home," I remarked.

"Home."

I found comfort in Jarvis's whispered echo. I heard him inhale deeply and follow it with a long exhale as if his lungs would collapse. He may have been homesick or completely taken by the night sky; though I knew his visibility was greatly restricted by the narrow canyon walls.

"Can you see Andromeda?" I quietly asked Jarvis.

"No. I can see her mother, Cassiopeia. She and her husband, Cepheus, have decided to save their kingdom by sacrificing Andromeda. She is chained to a rock at the edge of the sea. Can you see Andromeda, Jared?"

"Yes, I can. What will happen to her?" I begged an answer from Jarvis. Anything to keep him engaged.

"She needs Perseus to save her from the sea monster Cetus."

"Will Perseus arrive in time?"

~

Being fully exposed to the morning sun, I woke up first. I was terribly thirsty, but the camelback was in the cave, and neither of them was awake as far as I could tell. I quietly walked away to relieve what little I could. Not much. I was lightheaded, and my muscles were screaming. I made my way back to the rim.

"Jarvis," I called quietly.

"Jared?"

"How are you doing?"

"I do not like it here. It smells bad. I am running out of room." I knew what he meant. He had covered the walls and ceiling with numbers and constellations. I could only imagine.

"How's Angie?"

"Angelica Orabelle Havens is not well. I am afraid Perseus did not come to save her last night."

I had to get them out of there. When I left the day before, I knew Angie was in need of immediate medical attention. I could only imagine how dire her condition had become overnight. I was fairly certain she would not survive another day. I was also concerned about Jared. He had been off his meds for three full days.

I considered my options:

1. Climb back into the cave to evaluate her. *Not a good choice. My chances of making it back into the cave were slim to none. Then I would have to test fate for a third time as I tried to climb back out.*

2. Wait above the cave with hopes that the helicopters or the drone would make another pass. *It seemed they had crossed our location off their grid.*

3. Go back to the ravine, try to make my way to the canyon floor, and find my way back to the Zion Lodge, maybe Springdale.

"OK Jarvis, I have to go for help."

I could hear Angie stir with a soft moan. Jarvis began scratching on the wall on Angie's side of the cave. *Good. He's staying close to her.*

"Listen, Jarvis. You have to throw that bladder back up to me. But before you do, I want you and Angie to drink all of the water that is still in it. Wake Angie and make her drink. Got it?"

I could hear Jarvis trying to wake her. It sounded like she was disoriented. I could hear it in her voice.

"Suck on this. Suck on this, Angelica Orabelle Havens. Go ahead, suck on this." I could hear Jarvis repeat over and over as Angie forced herself awake. Any other time, Jarvis's directions would have doubled me over in disbelief and laughter. However, that day there was nothing humorous about it.

After they had sucked it dry, Jarvis tried launching it back up to me. Following my instructions, he held on to the straps I had connected together from his backpack and then attached to the camelback. I prayed it would hold. I caught it on the fifth or sixth try.

"Good job, Jarvis. I'm going to head out and refill this. I should be back in an hour or less."

Following the trail of small rock piles I had left the day before, I hiked across the rim in my battered bare feet and a pair of filthy stained shorts.

MATHIEU

I met Aidan at 6:30 the next morning. He looked like hell. If my memory served me right, and it usually did, he was wearing the same clothes he had worn the day before.

He must have been up all night making the necessary adjustments to the drone. Greeting him that morning, I prepared myself for his verbal lashing.

"Aidan, I don't know how to thank you."

"You can't. Let's just bring her home."

That went better than expected.

Aidan had met Angelica when I first started dating her. He was one of the first to say, *"Treat this one right; she's a keeper."* Those words came back to me. It was true. I knew after her drive on the first tee that I wanted to spend the rest of my life with her. I thought about her every minute of every day. I lavished her with expensive gifts and surprises. I took my time and treated her with the utmost respect rather than rushing her into my bed. I tried to include her in all of my family's affairs. I adored having her on my arm at fundraisers and PR events. She was at ease mingling with our guests, and she was raised to know all of the proper things to say and do. She looked exquisite in an evening gown. She was cute as hell in a T-shirt and a pair of pajama bottoms. She was stupendously photogenic no matter the occasion.

About two weeks into our developing relationship, she accompanied me to a crab feast and pool party at my parent's home. When she came out of the bathhouse in her bikini, I feared my reaction to her full figure and slender waist perched atop her long legs was going to look like Pinocchio's nose growing in the wrong hemisphere. Her natural beauty made the waiting next to impossible.

Aside from her physical attractiveness, it was the woman inside that instantly captivated me. In her, I had found someone that I wanted to love. I wanted to give her all of me and anything else her heart desired.

Then, she ran.

Aidan explained how he had removed the camera from the drone's underbelly and replaced it with a smartphone.

"It's the best audio solution I could come up with on such short notice. Hopefully, we'll find a signal and be able to maintain a connection with whoever we find out there."

"We'll be able to see them, and they'll see us?"

"Exactly."

"We'll be able to communicate?"

"That's the idea."

"Perfect." I slapped him on the back.

Much to Aidan's surprise, I suggested that we perform a quick test flight. I ran through the mud and residue left by the flood to the far side of the base camp. Aidan piloted the drone and sent it over to me. It hovered in front of my face enabling Aidan and I to hold a conversation while viewing each other.

"Genius, Aidan! Let's get her airborne."

For navigation, Aidan used the same toggles to maneuver the drone while watching his laptop LCD display for visual direction that was being provided by the onboard smartphone. It took us awhile to figure out how to steer it successfully around objects and obstacles. We brought it back several times to readjust the position of the smartphone until we felt we had the best angle to direct the small craft. Aidan had a second monitor to control its altimeter and artificial horizon. It was going to be tricky at best.

JARED

Within the hour, I returned with water and told Jarvis and Angie that it was time for me to try and make my way back to Zion Lodge.

"Jared?"

"Yes?"

"Don't go. Please, don't leave again."

"Angie, we have to get you out of that cave and to a hospital. There's no other way. If I make it down the ravine and onto the floor of the canyon, I'm sure I can make it back to the Lodge for help. I have to get you out of there. Do you understand?"

"But, you could get hurt... or worse. What good would that do?"

It could have been my imagination, but I thought I heard her crying. Jarvis remained quiet except for the scratching he had resumed on the cave's wall.

"Angie, I want you to know that no matter what happens, I'm glad we met. Hopefully, we'll all get home in one piece, and we can get together sometime. Would that be OK? Maybe you'll invite me to your wedding? How's that?"

"I will come to your wedding, Angelica Orabelle Havens," Jarvis chimed in much to my surprise. He hated social events.

"Jared, about my wedding... I'm not sure there's going to be a wedding."

Silence fell between us. My heart leapt at the thought that she might consider breaking her engagement. I knew it was wrong for me to revel in her despair. Breaking an engagement was nothing to think about casually, but neither was getting married. I had learned that the hard way. However, all of her thoughts and my reverie would be for naught if I didn't get her home.

"Angie, I have to go."

Her pleading became more intense.

"Jared, WAIT! I need to tell you something. Arrgh." She was breathing through her pain. She went silent, again.

"Angie? ... Jarvis, is she alright?"

"No."

"Jarvis, tell me what she's doing."

The stone Jarvis was using to scratch numbers and constellations into the walls of the cave went silent.

"Angelica Orabelle Havens, are you OK?" Jarvis asked her. He sounded like he was afraid of her.

"Yes, Jarvis. I'm going to be OK."

I breathed a sigh of relief. She spoke again.

"Jared, if you must go, know this: I ... I think ... I think I've fallen for you. I know that sounds horrible coming from someone who's supposed to be engaged, but ... Arrrgh... you have to stay safe. I just couldn't bear it if anything happened to you."

I was stunned by her admission. For days I had been fighting off my own feelings for her. Since the moment I first saw her in the airport, I had this need to be her protector, her guard. Now separated, she told me she had fallen for me. How I wished I were there to hold her and whisper my feelings for her against her lips. I wanted to tell her all that I had been holding in since our first hike into the Grand Canyon.

"Angie, we're going to make it out of here alive, all three of us. Got it? And when we get back east, we are going to get together and have the biggest damn party ever. You and I are going to get shitfaced drunk, and I am going to give you the dance of your life. Hear me?"

I could hear her laughing and coughing.

"I may never dance on this foot again, Jared."

"Yes. Yes, you will. And then I'll spin you around and I will kiss you, hard, then soft and tender, and then you'll know what I've always wanted to tell you."

Before responding, I could hear her breathing through a wave of pain.

"I would like that. I would like that very much."

I wanted to climb back into the cave. The thought of dancing with her and kissing her made what little blood I had rush through my veins. If only I could kiss her lips once before I left for that dreadful ravine; just once before we were rescued or found dead; just once before she was returned home and reconnected with her feelings for Mathieu Dufour.

Jarvis cleared his throat. It was his way of reminding us that he was still there. He always had a way of destroying memorable moments. At least Angie found him humorous. It was another thing that I loved about her.

"Angie, I fell for you the first time I saw you. You were being patted down by security at Philadelphia International Airport."

"You saw that?"

"I knew it!" Jarvis came alive again.

"Yes, you caught my eye immediately."

I could hear her breathing through her pain.

"After our climb up Bright Angel Trail, I knew the way I felt was undeniable. I knew it was wrong, but undeniable. I just couldn't stop..."

"Jared..." She was straining to speak.

I heard Jarvis mutter something about Andromeda.

"Angie, I'm going for help. We'll get you out of there and..."

I didn't know what to say next. I wanted to tell her that I loved her, and I would give my life for her. I wanted to confess that it was the memory of her smile that would keep me safe during my descent to the canyon floor. I closed my eyes and imagined a kiss, a real kiss - the kind of kiss that buckles a girl's knees and leaves a boy desiring more. I listened as her sobbing faded into silence.

"Angie?"

She did not respond.

"Jarvis? Is she OK? What's she doing?"

"Her eyes are closed. I think she's sleeping."

"Is she breathing?"

"I think so."

"JARVIS! Make sure. Is she breathing? Is she OK?"

Jarvis slid closer to her.

"Jarvis? How is she?"

"She's breathing."

"I'm going for help, Jar. I will get you guys out of there if it kills me."

"Don't die, Jared. You're my only good friend. I don't want to be alone."

"You're my only good friend, too, Jarvis. You take care of yourself while I'm gone. OK? Keep sipping the water. I'll be back."

"OK, Jared."

"Keep her safe. Do your best to keep her alive."

"I will Jared. I will take good care of Angie... I mean Angelica Orabelle Havens."

For a brief moment, he had felt something for Angie, too. He had called her by her first name, her preferred familiar name, something he reserved only for Mom; Dad, when he was around; and me.

"But you have to hurry, Jared. I think she is dying. I will give her a pillow. I will keep her warm. I promise."

"Good, Jarvis. Is the camelback near by?"

"Yes."

"Make sure you both drink plenty of water. Stay hydrated. I'll go get help."

"I love you, Jared. Will you tell Mom I love her, too?"

My heart was bursting. It was all too much.

"You make sure you tell her yourself when you get out of there. OK? "

"OK."

My heart broke. My whole world was trapped in a cave on the underside of a canyon wall. I had to find help or they would die, and then I would surely wish to die a thousand deaths more."

MATHIEU

We were ready. Aidan had mastered watching the smartphone and his instrument panel on a laptop while working the controls. We had lift off.

"I'd rather get it above the rim before we try taking it across the canyon. Maybe we can find that guy again. What's his name?" Aidan spoke as the drone climbed.

"Jared Lawson."

"Yeah, him."

We listened and watched as the drone rose straight up and reached an altitude 200 – 300 feet above the rim of the Canyon. Carrying the activated smartphone with it, Aidan started moving it toward the Temple of Sinawava.

The drone slowly vanished from our sight. Some thirty minutes later, Aidan had maneuvered it to the spot where we had located Jared Lawson the day before. He slowly spun it around 360 degrees several times.

"Nothing. No one," Aidan whispered. "Without a wide-angle camera lens, this is going to be more difficult than I thought. Our field of vision has been severely compromised. Hopefully, we'll be able to maintain a signal."

"Just keep moving across the rim. We've got to find him. Better yet, we've got to find Angelica."

Aidan stuck with it. He was tired, and I could tell fatigue was setting in. The craft was doing what he had aptly designed it to do. However, Aidan was wearing down.

JARVIS

Jared was my only good friend. Jared loved Angelica Orabelle Havens. She was very sick. She was very hot. Not like that. Her skin was very hot. She was sleeping. She was shaking. Therefore, I knew she was not dead. She did not smell good, and neither did I. She did not pee anymore. Her foot was very gross. My shirt was wrapped around it. My shirt was very gross. There were flies on it.

"Very Gross."

Jared went for help. We waited. It was getting very hot. Jared would be our Perseus. The heat was making me very tired of waiting for Perseus. Cetus the sea monster was coming for Andromeda.

JARED

Being able to confess the way I felt about Angie and hearing her admission gave me the resurgence of energy that I needed. I knew my feelings for her would last forever, but my energy level had its limits and wouldn't last long in the heat. I needed to make the best use of my time. First, I made my way back to the water source. It was a shallow spring-fed pool about a quarter mile from the cave. I drank heartily and splashed water all over my face and body. The cold water reminded me that I was still alive. How I had wished Jarvis and Angie were there with me to splash and drink in that emerald pool of life-giving water. There was no time to waste daydreaming. I had to make the trek back to the ravine. I walked with prayers on my lips and thoughts of them in my heart.

About two miles from the pool and many rock piles later, I found the ravine. I walked in either direction to see if I could find an easier descent into the canyon. There was none. My bare feet were scarred from the scramble up the canyon wall five days before. Perhaps it would be easier going down. I said one last prayer and began my descent.

MATHIEU

We were running out of battery life. We would have to scrap the mission soon and bring the drone back to base to reinsert another fully charged smartphone.

My father came up behind me and placed a hand on my shoulder.

"Any luck, gentlemen?"

"No." I exhaled heavily.

"The boys' mother is here. Would you like to meet her? I think she'd like to see you."

"Sure. Bring her in." I turned to Aidan. "Bring the drone back to base, load up another smartphone, and prepare to send her back out."

Aidan nodded. I think knowing that the mother had arrived gave him reason to comply without question.

I left the tent, walked out into the sunlight, and immediately recognized Mrs. Clara Lawson. I extended my hand.

"Mrs. Lawson, I'm Mathieu Dufour. How was your flight out?"

Her eyes were red with worry and framed with dark circles that weren't evident in the file photos that Garrison had sent.

"It was very nice. It was so kind of your family to make these arrangements for me. I don't know how I can ever thank you."

"Well, you're very welcome. However, I do wish we had better news for you."

"What? Is my son OK? Have you located my other son? What's happened?"

"Please, follow me, Mrs. Lawson."

I escorted her back into the tent and pulled up a folding chair for her.

"Here, please, sit down." Once she was seated, I proceeded with an update.

"Yesterday we located your eldest son, Jared. We sent a helicopter out to pick him up, but by the time they got to the site, he was gone. We had the drone out this morning, but we have not been able to find him. The good news is: he is well enough to move around and quite far, apparently. The bad news is: there's a lot of territory out there to cover. We had two helicopters and a drone up this morning. We'll keep searching. In the meantime, how can we make you more comfortable? Would you like some water, coffee? Would you be more comfortable in Springdale until we locate them?"

"Mr. Dufour, I understand your fiancée is missing, too. Is that correct?"

"Yes."

"I understand she was traveling with my sons. Is that true?"

"Yes. It appears they had been traveling together." For some unexplained reason I was disturbed that Mrs. Lawson was aware of all that.

"But there's been no sighting of her or my other son, Jarvis?"

"No ma'am, we haven't been able to locate either of them."

"Have you found any of the other missing people?"

"No, not with the choppers or the drone." I did not want to tell her that bodies had been found washed up down river from where we had last seen her son.

"Oh, dear God."

"Mrs. Lawson, we are doing our best."

The poor woman broke into tears. I could understand her fear and frustration. I understood her need to be with her sons, her need to know where they were and what was happening to them. I knew her desire for their safety. I stepped toward her and took her hands in mine. She rose from her chair, embraced me, and cried. Her body shook as she tried to withhold the wail that was building inside her. I felt her sadness come over me. Our chances of finding them alive were growing very slim. It was going on day 5 and I, too, had to consider that I might never see Angelica alive again.

JARED

The ravine was steeper than I thought. I was about twenty to thirty feet below the rim when I became painfully aware that I had run out of solid hand grabs and footholds. I would have to abort my descent, climb back up the wall, and look for another way down.

I was beyond frustration. Jarvis and Angie were back in the cave, perhaps dying. I prayed suffering would not send its misery upon them. I knew Angie was already being brave. She had mastered the art of hiding it from us. If she began to lose her fight, how would that effect Jarvis? Would he know how to help her, or would he panic? Without his meds, would he be able to handle the stress? I didn't want to lose either one. I could not let that happen.

They had enough water for one day. I calculated I had time to try one more descent. If I failed again, I would have to find my way back to the cave and then turn back out with the camelback to retrieve more water before nightfall.

To be honest, the thought of returning to the cave frightened me. I feared what I might find. What if no one answered me?

I climbed harder and faster. I heard a helicopter nearing my position. I looked up. Searching the sky, I lost my grip and my feet started to slide. I tried and failed to regain my balance. Shit!

MATHIEU

Aidan poked his head into the tent and interrupted our embrace. "Mathieu, we're ready to launch again."

Mrs. Lawson, still holding on to my sleeve, begged to come and watch with us. I looked over at Aidan.

"Sure."

The drone launched without a hitch. That much we had down. Navigating the uncharted territory was difficult and painstakingly slow. Mrs. Lawson stood behind us. I was not sure she could see much of anything, but for her it was better than standing around doing nothing while the ones she loved were in trouble. That much I understood.

The drone "Angelica" moved above the trees with the smartphone angled down about 45 degrees to cover the ground. We hovered above an opening and noticed what we had observed in several other places the day before and again that morning. I left the tent to intercept a park ranger and ask him about the pile of stones and rocks that appeared to mark a trail.

"Wait, Mathieu! I think we've picked him up again!"

I rushed back into the tent and rubbed my fatigued eyes that had been momentarily assaulted by the intense sunlight outside.

Aidan described the sighting as he maneuvered the drone. "I heard a flock of birds take flight like they had been stirred up, and look what I found."

The drone was closing in on a bare chested man crawling up and over the rim. He was badly scraped up. It looked like he had taken a nasty fall. He had a facial contusions and a shadow that was several days old. His hair looked greasy and his body glistened with sweat and grit. He slowly got to his feet, covered his eyes from the sun's glare, and stared at the drone as it approached.

"It's him! It's Jared!" Mrs. Lawson started screaming his name. "Jared! Jared!"

"Mom? Is that you?" He looked dazed and once again showed the signs of dehydration that Dr. Roberts had pointed out the day before.

"Mom?"

I yelled to one of the circling rangers to get the doctor back to our tent. A flurry of activity began mounting behind us as word got out and around the base that we had located "the survivor."

The drone moved closer, and Jared was able to see the screen. We moved his mother in view of the laptop camera so he could see her.

"Mom, where are you?"

"I'm here, Jared. I'm in Zion. We've been looking for you. Oh God, it's so good to see you. Where is Jarvis, is he OK?" His mother looked back at me. "Where is Angie, honey? Do you know where they are?"

"Yes. They are in a cave about two miles back. It is in the side of the canyon wall. Jarvis is OK, but Angie is in bad shape, Mom. I'm afraid she may die if we don't get her out of there soon."

Gasps and cheers went up. Feet began moving outside the tent upon hearing that the other two were still alive. I did not wait for Mrs. Lawson to respond to her son. I moved her away from the laptop.

"Jared, this is Mathieu Dufour."

Jared's mouth drew a tight line and his eyes penetrated our visual feed. Was it hatred, or was he studying me?

"Mathieu, she's dying. You have to get her out of there."

"How do we get there?"

"The cave is about two miles north. It's about 30 feet below the rim. The canyon's very narrow there. The walls are only about 20 to 30 yards apart."

"Too narrow for a chopper..."

"Too narrow for a chopper, but not too narrow for a lowered sling or basket."

"OK."

I picked up my walkie-talkie and told dispatch to get the choppers redirected. I gave them approximate coordinates based on Jared's directions and location. The second chopper was instructed to go directly to Jared and pick him up.

"I'm going back to the cave," Jared announced.

"No! Stay where you are. We'll come to you and airlift you out."

"No. I'm not leaving them." He was defiant.

"Then we'll airlift you to the cave. But you have to stay out of the way."

"Follow me. I'm no use in a helicopter. On the ground, I can get you there and help lower the gear."

"In the chopper, you can direct us, and we can get you there faster."

"I have to be the first one lowered down into the cave. There is no way you can send someone in there without me being there first."

Mrs. Lawson put her hand on my shoulder. I jerked my head around. *Why am I having an argument with this Lawson guy? Why doesn't your son just follow orders?*

"He's worried about his brother," Mrs. Lawson interjected as if she could hear my thoughts.

"Mrs. Lawson, I don't care what he's worried about. We don't have time to play his games. Angelica could be dying up there. Your sons will just have to suck it up."

"My son cares about her, too. He wouldn't be asking if he didn't think it best for both of them." Her stare was threatening.

"Then we go without him."

Jared Lawson bolted. I forgot that he could hear us and that was all he needed.

"Follow him! Don't lose him, Aidan."

Jared ran across the rim and headed due north as he had said.

"Get those choppers into that airspace, dammit. Pick up this guy, and get him the hell out of the way!" Admittedly, I was a mad man. He was putting Angelica's rescue at risk.

"No!" his mother screamed. "He can help you. He's leading you back to the cave."

"Not like this he isn't. He's going to lose us. We can't fly the drone through terrain like this. If we lose him, we might not be able to pick him up again."

Aidan was at the controls doing his best to stay right behind Jared. Guiding the drone around rock formations and through the scrub to stay on Jared's heels, Aidan whooped and hollered. Our chase had become some sort of a sick video game.

Five minutes into the flight, we heard a loud crack, and everything went black. I heard the sounds of afternoon hot bugs and a breeze rustling past the phone's speaker, but we had lost all visual contact.

"Fuck!" Aidan yelled. "She's down. That's it. You only get to crash her once. Show's over, folks. You can all go home."

Aidan casually tossed the controller in a fit of exhausted resignation.

"No!" Mrs. Lawson wailed.

"Try to launch it, Aidan. You've got to try!" I implored.

Aidan bent down and picked up the controller.

"C'mon, baby. Give us a little juice."

We could hear the motor humming, but it quickly became evident that the rotors had been sheared off. The "Angelica" was grounded. Her crash site was somewhere out there on the rim of Zion Canyon."

"Fucking asshole," I yelled, implicating Jared Lawson.

Mrs. Lawson lost it. "Dear God, what'll we do? We can't just leave them out there."

"Who are you calling an asshole?"

I turned back to the screen. To my disbelief, Jared had turned around, picked up the drone, and was speaking directly into its smartphone. We could not see him, but we could hear each other.

"You know, we could have saved your little drone if you'd just done it my way in the first place." He snarled sarcastically.

"Jared, just take us to the goddam cave. Can you do that please? We can get the exact location from the phone."

"I'm going to do just that. But you've got to watch your mouth, Dufour."

"Sorry. Just get us there."

The doctor arrived in the tent, thank God, and talked to Jared as he headed back to the cave with the smartphone in his hand. As Jared described Angie's condition, we could hear the two choppers in the background. One was staying on Jared; the other was working its way up the canyon. They had lowered an EMT in a harness, positioning him about 30 feet below the rim. Hoping he would spot the cave opening, they slowly moved the rescuer forward between the narrow canyon walls. The whole process was taking forever. Jared estimated he was approximately 2 miles from the cave when we had found him. Insuring the safety of its crew and its dangling team member, the helicopter continued moving up the canyon at a snail's pace.

Inside the tent, the doctor stayed on the line with Jared. Everyone else, except for Jared's mother, paced.

Treasuring the sound of her son's voice, she remained at the doctor's side.

Finally, a ranger rushed into our tent.

"They found the cave. They are preparing to send Cole in, and then they'll lower a basket."

"Oh. Thank. God."

CHAPTER FIFTEEN

JARVIS

I heard a helicopter. It was moving up the canyon. I moved Angelica Orabelle Havens' head off my shoulder. She did not wake up. I was scared. I waved and yelled. A man came flying up the canyon. He was harnessed to a cable. The cable was attached to the helicopter. He saw me. He handed me a pole, and I pulled him in. He was very brave. He said I was very brave, too. I went to Angelica Orabelle Havens. I told her that help had arrived. She did not hear me. The helicopter sent a basket down, and the man grabbed the basket with a hook. I helped him move Angelica Orabelle Havens into the basket. I wanted to go with her. He said she was sleeping. He said I could not go. I had to wait. I wanted to cry when Angelica Orabelle Havens left. I did not get to say good-bye. Then I had to wait in the cave with the man.

"I said I would take good care of her... I promised."

He said his name was Stephen Cole Townsend, but his friends called him Cole. He said that he had been an EMT for ten years. I heard the helicopter fly away with Angelica Orabelle Havens. I was stuck in the cave with Stephen Cole Townsend the EMT. He was not Perseus. Jared, my brother and only good friend, was Perseus. He led them to the cave. Stephen Cole Townsend said they were taking Angelica Orabelle Havens to a hospital. Actually, he said "Angelica." He did not say "Orabelle Havens." He said Angelica would get the best care there.

"I cared..."

Stephen Cole Townsend called for the second helicopter. He said they needed to get me out. He asked about my numbers and constellations on the walls. I told him about Andromeda and her mother, Cassiopeia. I told him Perseus would come and save her. I do not think that Stephen Cole Townsend was listening. He said nothing. He took pictures of the walls and ceiling.

A second helicopter hovered over the cave. Stephen Cole Townsend pulled in another cable. He said it was my turn to go for a ride. He said the helicopter would take me to the hospital. He wanted me to get into a harness. He had to attach his harness to mine. He was too close. He was touching me. I could not breathe.

"I cannot do this! I cannot do this!"

Stephen Cole Townsend stabbed me.

JARED

I was about a half mile from the cave when I watched the second helicopter raise Jarvis in a basket. His body was limp and lifeless. Something was wrong. There was no way my brother would have allowed them to confine him and then swing him above the canyon floor in a basket. Something had gone terribly wrong. I was too late.

"What happened to Jarvis?" I yelled at the drone's smartphone as I tried to pick up my pace. "You told me Angie was being airlifted to a hospital and that Jarvis was in good health. What the hell happened?"

"They had to subdue him, Jared. He became violent. He was putting everyone at risk. There was no other way," the doctor tried to calmly explain.

"He's going to be OK," my mother chimed in from the background.

"That's why I told them to do it my way."

Straining to watch Jarvis make his ascent toward the helicopter, I looked up while running across the edge of the rim. I saw a hand reach out to pull him in. That was when I hit loose dirt. My ankle twisted and I fell.

"OH. SHIT!"

ANGIE

I was wearing a white gown that flowed around my ankles. Jared was in a pair of distressed jeans that were frayed around the cuffs and shredded at the knee. Showing off his sun-kissed chest, his long-sleeve white linen shirt was left completely unbuttoned and haphazardly tucked in at the waist. All showered and clean-shaven, he was so handsome and happy. So was I! Suspended above an emerald pool of water and dancing in our bare feet, we appeared to be weightless. Spinning me around, laughing, and kissing me, he led me in his strong arms. Intentionally, he dropped into the deep cold water and pulled me in with him. Still laughing, we surfaced together. I splashed him. He dove under and came up beneath me. He lifted me up and onto his shoulders only to dunk me right back down into the water again. When I surfaced for air, he gathered me up, smiled, and then gently assaulted my lips. Our bodies began to swirl around in the water, and our legs were wrapped around each other. We were completely naked, and I could feel his desire for me on my inner thigh. I tilted my head back as he moved his lips and tongue down my wet neck. His lips...

"Angie? Hi!" I heard a whisper. It was not Jared. It was a voice much different from his.

MATHIEU

We lost contact with Jared, again. He was running along the rim with the smartphone in his hand when suddenly we lost him. The drone was unresponsive and pronounced dead. Aidan was wrong; we got to crash it twice.

The helicopter that delivered Angelica to the University Trauma Center in Las Vegas refueled and was sent back out to search again for Jared. Headed for his last known coordinates, a ground team was sent out on foot. There was nothing more for Aidan and me to do.

Aidan was taken to a local hotel for a well-deserved rest, and I went on to the hospital to finally be reunited with Angelica. My parents drove, Mrs. Lawson sat in the middle seat, and I slept in the "way-back" of the rented SUV.

At the hospital, Mrs. Lawson was taken to a wing on the first floor to be with her younger son. We were intercepted and escorted up to the ICU to join Angelica's parents in a designated waiting room.

Angelica's parents had arrived in Springdale the morning before and then sped off to Las Vegas as soon as they had learned their daughter was being airlifted. Their postures and faces told us that the news was not good. Her father walked me out into a deserted hallway. There, he bravely told me that Angelica would lose her left foot above her ankle, at the very least.

"But she's going to be OK, right? She will survive, right?" I clutched his arm. I needed reassurance that we had rescued her in time to save her.

"It will be touch and go. One day at a time. If she survives the first couple of days, she will have greater challenges ahead. Mathieu, we cannot thank you enough."

CHAPTER SIXTEEN

ANGELICA

"Oh Mommy! It's really you!" The room slowly came into focus. Everything was bright and drenched in white. I was lying on an actual bed. I had luscious warm blankets covering my body. My throat was scratchy and raw. My head was fuzzy. Brushing her soft hand over my forehead, my mother smiled at me. Her eyes were heavily rimmed. She was a beautiful sight.

"We were so afraid we'd lost you. But you're here. You're safe now."

I saw my dad standing behind her. As soon as I locked eyes with him, he choked back a sob. He leaned over and kissed my forehead.

"Where are Jared and Jarvis? Did they make it out? Are they OK?"

My mom brushed my cheek, and then she rested her hand on my arm. Something was wrong. They were not telling me everything. My concern rewrote the look on her face. I felt it in the quiver of her fingers on my skin.

"Jarvis is here in the hospital. He's going to be fine. His mother tells me he might be discharged tomorrow or the next day."

"You met his mother?"

"Yes, darling. She's wonderful. She was asking for you, too."

"And Jared? Where's Jared?"

My mother looked back to my father with her all too familiar "How should I spin this?" look. My dad stepped up to the bed and kissed my cheek.

"Hi, Angel. Jared will be fine."

"Where is he?" I demanded to know.

"He led the rescue team to you and Jarvis. They are out there now working to pick him up and bring him out."

"So they know where he is?"

"They have a good idea. He should be out of the canyon soon."

Trying to read my thoughts, my mother looked into my eyes. So much pain was swirling within her dark pupils. I could only imagine what Jared's mother must have been going through.

"I would like to meet Mrs. Lawson. Do you think that would be possible?" I asked.

My poor mother nodded her head in consent as a tear drifted down her cheek.

"It's OK, Mommy. It will be over soon. They'll find Jared. He's a very smart man. He will find the rescue team, and they will bring him out. I'm sure of it."

My mother smiled back at me.

A man in a white coat with an oversized name badge and stethoscope approached my bed. Before my parents stepped aside, my father made the introduction.

"Honey, this is Dr. Olenski. He needs to speak with you."

The doctor nodded, moved to the side of my bed and took my hand. There was more news; I could see it in my parents' eyes and the way they were braced against each other as if they were under attack.

"Angelica, I'm your surgeon, Dr. Olenski. When you arrived at the hospital, your ankle and several bones in your foot were shattered. Do you remember that?"

I nodded, "Yes." As he spoke, I was relieved that my pain was gone. I tried to move my numbed leg. Yes, the pain was gone. But something felt wrong and unbalanced. Tears were flowing from my mother's eyes as my father clutched her hand.

The doctor continued. "You developed sepsis, Angelica. It's a real miracle you're alive. However, we couldn't save your foot." The doctor continued talking as my mind tried to process what he was saying. Something about septic shock and the severity of pain I must have been in...

"MY DANCE! I WANT MY DANCE! HE PROMISED ME A DANCE!" my head was screaming, but to those standing beside my bed, they could not hear my words, only my wailing. I could not look. If I looked, then it would be real.

"TAKE MY FOOT? I'LL SHOW YOU. I'LL JUMP OUT OF THIS BED AND SHOW YOU MY FOOT!" my head continued screaming in denial.

I began to throw off my covers, and I tried to swing my legs over the side of the gurney. The doctor and a nurse grabbed my shoulders and held me. I felt the tangle of tubes and wires pulling at my body. Then, I looked down.

I am certain my screams could be heard in the next wing.

MATHIEU

Her parents reported that when the surgeon told her about her amputation, she became violent and tried to rip out her IVs and monitors. The surgeon feared she would hurt herself and ordered that Angelica be sedated. Apparently, during the melee, she also made it abundantly clear that she did not want to see me, either.

Her mother assured me that Angelica was receiving the best care and prevailed upon me to be patient and to give her time. The doctor said her reaction was not uncommon and that I should not take it personally or try to read too much into it. She was going through a radical change and needed time. Because Angelica was having difficulty in recovery, my parents did not have the opportunity to see her before they said their goodbyes and rushed off.

"There is no way for any of us to know what she is going through. I can't even begin to imagine." My dad tried to encourage me, and then he gave me a manly hug.

"Please give her our love," Mom said as she kissed my cheek and then waved goodbye.

Oh, how I wish I could.

I felt abandoned.

Once she learned that Angelica had been rescued, Camille caught the first evening flight out. I had a limo meet her at the airport and take her to her hotel for the night. She found me in the waiting room the following morning.

"How's she doing?"

I told her as much as I knew.

CAMILLE

He was so broken up and lost. Never had I seen a man so vulnerable as Mathieu was then. He absolutely worshipped Angie. He had spent the last three months courting her the way every man should. They were inseparable until the day she left for Las Vegas.

He had not eaten anything in days. I did not have to ask; I could tell. He was losing weight and beginning to look drawn. I did manage to get him to drink a cup of coffee and a bottle of water that morning. I thought I had come to Nevada to see Angie; but apparently, it was Mathieu who needed me the most. I stayed with him through the morning. Finally, he received word that Angie was awake and asking for him. Mathieu rose, took a deep breath, and followed the nurse.

"I hope he's ready for this," I overheard Angie's mother mutter.

MATHIEU

She smiled when I peered around the doorframe. Her dimples caused my heart to leap with the joy she had always given me. Rushing to her bedside, I was flooded with relief.

"Oh Angel, I have missed you so much." I took her hands in mine, raised them to my lips, and gently kissed them. My worst fears were finally allayed. My ring was on her finger and it sparkled in the bright overhead lights of her private room. *"My Angel..."*

"Please, don't ever run from me again. I won't survive it a second time. Whatever it is that I've done, I will fix it."

I laid my head down on her hands still held in mine. She slipped one of her hands out from my grip and gently stroked my hair.

"I'm so sorry," she whispered. Her voice was very strained and weary. "I never meant to hurt you."

"Hurt me? Angel, please don't apologize or consider consoling me. It is you we need to take care of. For God's sake, let me be wherever you are. Let me take care of you."

I stood on my feet and moved over her to place a tender kiss on her lips. Hers were still sore and cracked from the dehydration she had suffered. After our lips touched briefly, I pulled back and studied her eyes.

"Mathieu, they had to amputate my leg." At first, she was very matter-of-fact about it. However, as I knelt beside her, she began to break down. Her lower lip quivered as tears began streaming from the corners of her eyes and onto her pillow.

"It's all right, Angel. It's going to be all right. We'll work through this together." I leaned toward her ear. "You're here. You're alive. That's what's important. We'll get through this. OK?"

"Yes. And Mathieu..."

"Yes, Angel?"

"I won't be running from you anytime soon," she cast an eye toward her missing limb.

"That's my girl." I kissed her forehead. We laughed at her little joke. Then she started crying again. I crawled up onto the hospital gurney and held her. Angelica quietly cried herself to sleep in my arms.

"I love you, Angelica. I will always love you. Always and forever."

At some point in time, a nurse had entered the room and found us both curled up and asleep. She quietly closed the curtains and turned out the lights.

ANGIE

It had been a week since I started my hike along the floor of Zion Canyon. Almost swept away, I would not have survived the flash flood had it not been for Jared and Jarvis. I knew Jarvis was safe and due to be released from the hospital. Jared had not been found, as yet. Mathieu assured me that the search teams were covering every inch of the rim. Mathieu, Aidan, and Jared's mother were the last people to see Jared via the smartphone attached to the drone that Aidan had built.

Mathieu told me how he and Aidan had worked tirelessly until they had found me. He said the drone had crashed but the helicopters were still in the air searching for Jared. He said that Jared was the problem because he would not stay in one place, and he added that Jared almost jeopardized my own rescue. Fortunately, they were able to locate the cave, anyway.

Once Mathieu had permission to visit my room, he rarely left my side. The nurses brought in a cot, blanket, and pillows for him. My parents were able to get a hotel room and were in to see me every morning, afternoon, and night.

~

When my parents arrived the second morning, Mom said she'd seen Jarvis's mother in the cafeteria and learned that Jarvis was due to be released that afternoon.

"Before they leave, I'd like to see Jarvis to thank him, and I'd like to say goodbye to Mrs. Lawson," Mathieu thought out loud. "I'm going to go down to the cafeteria. Maybe she will still be there. Anyone need anything?"

"Yes! Would you please ask Jarvis and Mrs. Lawson to stop by my room before they leave? I'd like to see them, too."

I knew Mathieu would deliver the message. I knew he would make it happen. Despite Jared's apparent insurrection, Mathieu said he was grateful for his attempts to get help and to Jarvis for pulling me out of the canyon.

I closed my eyes and recalled Jared's shocked face when he first saw me in Zion, and how he and Jarvis dragged me up the steep wall ahead of the rushing torrent of water. I could still hear Jared tenderly asking me if I was going to be OK. I recalled how he coaxed me into peeing over the back ledge of the cave for the first time; the way he made me laugh, relax, and finally pull it off. I chuckled to myself thinking of how Jarvis would have literally interpreted the phrase "pull it off." I remembered the feel of Jared curled up behind me to keep me warm, how his arm circled my waist, and how my fingers naturally laced through his. I remembered how I felt him kiss the back of my head when he thought I was asleep. I thought of how he made sure I had water to drink and constantly checked my forehead for my temperature. I remembered how he promised we would celebrate when we got back to the East Coast. I remembered his laugh. I remembered his whispers of encouragement. I remembered the prayers Jared said for me. He also prayed for his brother, our parents, and even one for Mathieu. If only I could hear his whispers once more.

I said a prayer for Jared. It seemed God was the only one who knew where his was. It had been two days since I left the canyon and still no word or sightings. I was beginning to fear the worst. I could not imagine what his mother and brother were going through. I felt out of touch with those who had come to matter most to me. I did not know what the weather was like at night, and I hated the thought that Jared was spending his nights cold and alone, perhaps badly injured or suffering. The thought of him still out there, somewhere, dying a slow death was more than I could bear.

It was probably unfair of me to ask Mrs. Lawson and Jarvis to stop by before they left the hospital. It was possible that his mother would rather not see me. After all, I was the one her sons stayed to rescue. They risked their lives to save mine, and now Jared, the one who sacrificed so much to care for his brother and me, was left behind. I silently held back my tears as my heart sank with grief. I had fallen hard. I knew it then. I knew it all too well.

I needed to see Jarvis. He was my last connection to Jared.

MATHIEU

I found Mrs. Lawson in the cafeteria. She was alone, sipping her coffee, and staring at a wall of windows on the far side of the room.

Trying not to startle her, I placed my hand on her frail shoulder and whispered, "Mrs. Lawson?"

"Mathieu, how good to see you again." She reached up and took my hand.

I sat down next to her. Like one would when addressing a frightened child, I wanted to speak with her at eye level.

"How is Jarvis?"

"He is doing much better, thank you. He should be discharged this afternoon. Thank you again for finding him and for flying me out here. I think it really helped to have me at his bedside when he woke up. How can I ever repay you?"

"Please, that's not necessary. Your sons took care of Angelica and made sure she was OK."

She patted my hand. "How is your fiancée?"

"She's going to be fine. She will be here for another week, maybe two."

"Jarvis has been very concerned about her. He said she is the most beautiful woman he has ever seen." There was a little spark in her eye. "He never notices things like that. He also said she was very brave and kind. She must be a very special person to catch the attention of my younger son."

I dropped my face and nodded my head in agreement.

"That she is, Mrs. Lawson. I don't know what I would have done if we had not found her and brought her out when we did. I would have launched an army or purchased my own fleet of choppers." I stopped there. The thought of not being able to find her was too much for me to revisit. "Any word on Jared?"

"No." She closed her eyes, squeezing a tear to the surface. It drifted down her cheek. "We're running out of time, aren't we?" She looked up at me with a lost and pleading stare.

I knew she wanted me to tell her that there was still time and that Jared would be found. However, the truth was, the chances of finding him alive were slim to none. I knew that any day they would move the mission from "search and rescue" to "recovery, " and when that happened, I also knew it would kill her. From the file Garrison, God rest his faithful soul, had assembled for me, I had noted that Mrs. Lawson was a divorcee with no immediate family members other than her sons. She would probably receive some support from the small business that employed her and the local church they attended. Other than that, she and Jarvis would be left to hold each other up.

I thought of Garrison and his family. My parents had returned home with his body. They called to say they had met his very pregnant wife and his extended family in a private hangar. My mother said that as the door to the jet was lowered, Mrs. Legrand was blessed to have her so many loved ones surrounding her. My mother described how Mrs. Legrand's two brothers caught their sister as she collapsed at the sight of her husband's casket being lowered from the jet by Garrison's own staff and my father. My parents said it was the most difficult thing they have ever had to endure. As I sat there with Mrs. Lawson, I wondered which would be worse: to learn of a loved one's death, or "not knowing."

ANGELICA

Camille arrived back at the hospital about an hour after my parents. She had never been an early riser. Once she entered my room, the world lightened up. She immediately went over to the window and raised the curtain announcing that it was a glorious day outside. She kissed my mom on her cheek and warmly accepted my dad's big bear hug. Mathieu gave her his trademark one-sided smile and shook his head incredulously at her unrestrained entrance. Thankfully, the nursing staff did not press our security breach. Only family members were supposed to be in my room and only two at a time.

Up until Camille arrived with a splash, everyone had been walking on eggshells, waiting for me to slip into a deep depression. Everyone except Camille, that is. She plopped herself down beside me on my bed and asked what adventures we were going to take that day.

Camille carried on like nothing had happened. She went on about some cute interns she had run into on her way up to my room. I was sure they had noticed her, too. Camille was very pretty in a cute sort of way. Her effervescent personality outshined her impossible bright eyes and full smile. She had a way of drawing people in with a single glance. It was good to have her near.

While Camille kept everyone engaged in conversation, nurses came in, took my vital signs, and checked my bandages. After being poked and prodded, I reclined and thought of Jared. Knowing that he was lost and in grave danger, I found it difficult to follow the conversations that were taking place in my room. I was disconnected from my visitors on so many levels. I had lost the lower part of my leg, and I knew it would be a long climb back; however, I didn't think I could survive losing Jared.

The morning hours drifted into early afternoon. People came and went from my room. I fell in and out of sleep.

I reveled at the arm that was wrapped around my shoulder and tenderly caressing me. I lifted my head and felt his warm breath on my forehead. He was breathing heavily, and I knew his invitation was the manifestation of his desire, spurring on my own for him. Our eyes were open in the dark confines of our surroundings, and I ever so slowly inched my face toward his. His lips were a magnet, and soon I would reach the point of no return. There was a thrill released in my body that sent chills through my stomach and into the lower reaches of my spine. I had to have him. My hand reached up to his broad shoulder and...

There was a commotion outside my door. It rudely jolted me from my very pleasant dream. I heard footsteps coming down the hall and Jarvis's loud voice. Startled by the realization that they were near, I quickly prepared myself to meet Mrs. Lawson and to see Jarvis one last time. I made sure nothing was falling out or exposed beneath the covers. You know how those hospital gowns are, and I wasn't convinced the steamy excitement of my dream had receded from my body. I had to pull myself together before they arrived.

A very dirty face peered around the corner.

"Jared? JARED!"

CHAPTER SEVENTEEN

MATHIEU

While visiting with Mrs. Lawson, she had received word that Jared had been rescued and that he was en route to the hospital. I had every intention of telling Angelica, but she was napping when I returned to her room. Shortly after that, Camille arrived like a live wire. I had to wait for the right moment. What I had not anticipated was Jared's speedy flight to the hospital and subsequent escape from the hospital ER staff. He made an awkward and untimely entrance into Angelica's room. Apparently, when Mrs. Lawson told him that Angelica was safe and recovering in ICU, he pulled out his IV, dashed out of the ER, and raced upstairs. Stunned by his actions, Jarvis and his mother gave chase through the hospital corridors. The commotion attracted the attention of everyone on both floors. With voices and footsteps bouncing through the halls and landing outside Angelica's door, the hospital seemed to be in chaos.

Jared paused. When their eyes met, they were oblivious to everyone else in the room. Angelica's dimples deepened as she broke the biggest smile I had ever seen. Jared rushed to the side of her bed, knelt down in his appalling state, and gushed.

"Thank God, you're alive! The very thought of you was the only thing that kept me sane. I knew you'd make back. We did it, Angie! We did it!"

"Yes, yes!" was all Angelica could say. She was overwhelmed. I watched in horror as their affection for one another became evident and played out in front of everyone.

With suspicious drama written all over her face, Camille looked over at me and cocked her head sideways.

Angelica and Jared sobbed while embracing each other. Jarvis and Mrs. Lawson stood in the doorway. Jarvis's eyes were averted while Mrs. Lawson appeared stunned. The room suddenly became very crowded. Angelica looked up and saw the other two Lawson family members.

"JARVIS! Come over here. I missed you!" Angelica waved him over. Nurses rushed past him, and scolded Jared for breaking away.

"Mr. Lawson, we need to get you back to the ER for your evaluation. This is highly irregular," one nurse admonished while another called for security. A doctor on the floor came in to help manage the situation.

As security approached him, Jared leaned over and kissed Angelica. I saw it coming, and fortunately, his lips went no farther than her forehead. The man was a smelly dirty mess and had no place in her room. As they escorted him out he yelled back.

"I love you, Angie!"

His eyes met mine. Incensed rage flowed through my veins. My fists were clenched. I wanted to deck him and thank him all at the same time. Then, deck him again to make myself clear.

Word leaked out to the media, and the event became one of those featured stories told in dramatic fashion on the network news journals. I was subjected to the retelling of their emotional reunion over and over again. Together, they had become a part of Zion history and rendered me powerless to erase what had happened between them.

ANGIE

It was true. I was not dreaming. We had said those things to each other in the canyon. Together, we went through hell and back, and our hell was the very thing that united us. Our suffering and struggle to stay alive was stronger than the destruction that had surrounded us. As I lay in my clean hospital sheets and gown in my sterile ICU room, Jared had made his way back to me carrying the scrapes, bruises, and the smell of death that tried to possess us in the cave. Only the three of us could possibly understand the bonding power of our suffering and the beauty in our scars. Jared was absolutely exquisite and ravishing in his victory! I wanted to hold him the way he had held me when I needed him. The feel of Jared's touch on my skin and the knowledge that he was safe lifted my spirit and gave me hope. With Jared safe, I could actually believe that I might have a future and that I could survive. Perhaps, I could thrive in the wake of all that had happened to us. If only for one brief magnificent moment, he was right there beside me. We had been reunited.

Jared was amicably removed from my room by hospital staff and taken back to the ER. He did not resist. The remainder of my day became a fog as an emotional charge lingered in my room. Mathieu never left my side, working hard to stabilize the environment. Seemingly oblivious to the significance of what had just transpired, Camille, my parents, doctors, and nurses came and went like ponies on a carousel. Everyone talked endlessly about the weather and how good it would be to get me home so I could begin my "new normal." I, on the other hand, wished they would all leave. Hoping the dust would settle around him soon, I waited impatiently for Jared to come back. On watch for his return, I kept my eyes on the door of my hospital room. I needed his smile. I needed him.

JARED

"Do you mind telling me what the hell just went on up there?" My mother was clearly upset. She almost never cursed. Those were the first words out of her mouth once we were back in the ER. Meanwhile, Jarvis was cheering me on. He was as excited for me as when I was scoring touchdowns in high school. My mother studied him as if he were an alien.

After I was caught in Angie's room, I was escorted back to the ER by two security guards, a doctor, and two nurses. My mother had quietly directed Jarvis to follow her. IVs were restarted, and monitors were reconnected. My heart sounded strong. My oxygen and BP levels were good. I was feeling better, much better. Angie looked great! She was happy to see me, and Jarvis, too. Her fiancé? Not so much. *You're welcome, too, asshole.* But sadly, Angie was still wearing his ring, and he was staked out in her room.

After things had settled down and the medical staff was convinced I would not bolt again, my family was left in peace.

"Jared, it's so good to see you. I was so scared they wouldn't find you." Saying my mother was relieved would have been a huge understatement. Jarvis was all smiles. He still avoided eye contact with me, but his ear-to-ear happiness was glued to his downward turned face and that was good enough for me.

Mom said that Jarvis had told her some of what had happened, but she wanted to hear more from me, especially regarding Angie and my last days alone at the bottom of the canyon. I told her as much as I could remember. I told her how I was racing back to the cave when they were airlifting Jarvis out. I described how I looked up, lost my balance, and fell, sliding down a wall of rock and debris. Once I regained my footing, my only choice was to work my way down to the floor. I must have fallen again, and quite a ways, because at some point in time I had lost consciousness. I left out the details regarding my fall for Angie. I left it to Jarvis to fill in those blanks.

"Jared likes Angelica Orabelle Havens," Jarvis blurted out.

"Jared, do you care to explain? That was a pretty big scene you made back there in Miss Havens' room."

I really did not want to talk about it.

"Jared," my mother was not going to let it go, "you do realize she's engaged?"

"Angelica Orabelle Havens should dump Mathieu Olivier Dufour," Jarvis answered for me.

My mother whipped her head around and stared at my brother like he had just robbed a bank.

"JARVIS!" she scolded, "Mr. Dufour is responsible for your rescue. His family flew me out here. He was sick with worry about Angelica…"

"Angie. She prefers to be called Angie, Mom. Mr. 'Du-four' would know that if he got off his high horse and paid enough attention," I interrupted.

"Jared, that's not fair. It's clear to me that he adores her. He worships the ground she walks on. "

"Then why did she run?" I challenged.

"What?"

"Why was she out there alone, more specifically, without her fiancé? Because she needed to get away and reevaluate everything," I was too quick to answer.

"That doesn't give you permission to move in!" My mother was fierce in her response.

It dawned on me then that there might have been more to my father's abandonment of his family than Jarvis's challenges. This discussion was obviously touching a raw nerve for my mom.

"I didn't mean for it to happen. It just did." Not wanting to face or defy all of the values my mother had instilled in me from a young age, I bowed my head.

"Jared, you need to let her go and allow her to finish what she set out to do. She's engaged. She made a promise. If you truly love her, you'll walk away and let her go."

"I don't think I can."

"You have to. Neither one of you will ever be sure if you don't allow her mission to play out to completion without your interference. Mathieu will always be in the back of her mind as a 'what if?' if you don't back away and let her work it through."

I knew my mother was right, and then she sealed her case.

"Jared, she's still wearing his ring. No matter what you want to believe, she's still committed to their

relationship. He is in her room 24/7. Didn't you notice
the cot? It's for Mathieu. He told me himself that he never
leaves her room."

"You spoke to him?"

"Of course I did. Just this morning he met me in the
cafeteria. He wanted to know how I was holding up. He
wanted to know how Jarvis was doing. He wondered if any
progress was being made in your rescue effort. He's not a
bad guy, Jared. He's a very likeable person. He deserves
your respect. They both deserve your understanding and a
speedy exit out of their lives."

"Angie said she loves Jared," Jarvis threw in as my
last defense.

"She did? Are you sure that's what she meant?"

"Yes. They slept together."

The defense rests its case.

ANGIE

I was weary. As long as I was there, Mathieu
intended to stay. He had taken an indefinite leave from the
winery. Stating that my wellbeing should be his first
priority, his parents assured him that they could manage
without him for several weeks. The Dufour family had gone
through great lengths and expense to find and remove me
from the canyon. I felt indebted to them, and my parents
were eternally grateful. Those sentiments weighed heavily
on my conscience.

Camille stayed through the weekend, and then she
headed for home. We did not have the opportunity to talk
alone about all that had happened, especially the details. I
was dying to tell her about what really went on inside the
cave. I wanted to tell her that while I thought I was going to
die no less than three times, I felt like I had found sanctuary
in Jared's strength and resolve. I wanted to tell her about
Jarvis. I wanted to tell Camille how he had pulled me up the

canyon wall. I wanted to tell her how endearing and brilliant Jarvis was. I wanted to tell her that I had fallen for his older brother.

True, the Dufours spared no expense in bringing us out. However, I knew I would never be able to convey how the steadfastness of the Lawson brothers gave me the will to survive and the desire to fight through the pain. The three of us thirsted, hungered, and fought our way out together. I would not have made it past the wall of water or the dark cold of the cave had it not been for Jared and Jarvis. I spent my days politely smiling while impatiently waiting and watching for Jared to return to my room.

On Sunday afternoon, Camille gave me a long hug prior to leaving for the airport. She was headed for home to prepare the house for my return. First, I would enter the Bryn Mawr Rehab Hospital in Paoli, Pennsylvania. It was known as one of the best rehab facilities in the country. Arrangements were being made for my flight and admittance.

Another day passed, and I continued to wait for Jared to revisit my room. By the third day, I became concerned about his wellbeing. Maybe his injuries were not apparent, and maybe he was in worse shape than I had originally surmised. Secretly, I panicked. I waited until Mathieu stepped out of my room, and out of desperation, I covertly begged my mother to inquire about Jared. That was how and when I learned that Jared had been discharged earlier that morning.

He did not stop in to say goodbye. He just checked out. In fact, I had not seen or heard from him after our initial reunion. If I did not know better, I would have said that Mathieu had something to do with it. Being the honorable man that Jared was, I thought it was also possible that he had decided it best not to cause another scene. He had probably come to his senses. After all, when he took my hands in his, I was still wearing my engagement ring. If he did not see it, he must have felt it when he rubbed his thumbs across the back of my knuckles. When I heard that he, Jarvis, and his mother were headed back east, I felt sick. I felt alone and forgotten. I sank into depression. Was it possible that he became disinterested when he learned of my amputation?

That was not the man that cared for me in Zion. Did I really know him at all?

I visited with a psychologist every day. I looked forward to our sessions. They were my one break from Mathieu. He was not permitted to attend. My doctor was focused on developing my skills and ability to cope with a missing limb. She tried to help me understand my grief over my loss. She gave me the professional and experienced insight that I needed. After I learned of Jared's departure, she noted my slip into deeper depression. It was then that I confessed my loss as being two-fold: I had lost my leg, but I also lost a person who I thought was the best man I had ever known. He was gone, swept away from me without explanation. Jared came crashing into my life like a hurricane and receded without notice like an ebb tide. Meanwhile, our story was playing out in the news. The world continued to spin, and the sun rose every day while I was left to cope without my lower leg, and without my heart that was carried away by a man I had only known for nine intense days. My phantom pain was immense.

At night, I dreamt that my leg was still there. I could run and dance. My legs were strong and agile in my dreams. Sometimes I would wake up after and feel its presence like it had never left, or it had miraculously returned to me. I would allow myself a few moments of remembrance before I looked and reconfirmed reality of my loss.

I dreamt of Jared, too. I was happy in my dreams of Jared. We were laughing. We were intimate. I would wake up and instantly know he was gone. I wanted to linger there and live in my dream world, but to no avail.

There were many times when I cried for no reason. It troubled me that I could not pinpoint the obvious. It should have been obvious, right? I had every reason to cry.

Was I grieving my leg as my doctor said I would? Was it Jared? Both?

Finally, during one of my crying jags, my mother asked Mathieu if he would leave the room so she could have some private time with me. Mathieu reluctantly honored her request and left. My mother and I whispered.

"Darling, I hate to see you in this much pain."

"I know, mom. I am so scared. I don't know if I can do this."

"You're a strong woman, Angie. And, it's OK if you have doubts. It's OK. You need to grant yourself the right to be frightened and to grieve. You have the right to miss what you've lost. Do you need more space and time alone?"

"Yes. No. I don't know. I don't know what I need."

I paused because, in truth, I did know.

"I need Jared." It felt good to say it out loud.

There was silence as my mother tried to absorb what I had just confessed.

"Mom?"

"Yes, Sweetheart."

"I don't know if I can do this without Jared, and Jarvis, too. They became a part of me, and I don't want to continue this journey without them. I don't know how it all happened, but it did. And now, I feel lost without them."

"I'm not surprised," my mom quietly sympathized. "They saved your life. You spent five grueling days together beating the odds. The three of you conquered challenges most people will never face in their lifetimes."

"Mom, it was more than five days and it's more than just a friendship when it comes to Jared."

She raised an eyebrow, but I knew she was not all that shocked. She was just surprised to hear me admit it.

"Judging by the way Jared stormed your room, I gathered something significant happened out there."

My mom stayed in Las Vegas while my father returned home. Hopefully, I would be able to make the trip in a week. My doctor was already working with his counterparts at Bryn Mawr Rehab.

My mother, bless her heart, spoke with Mathieu about my need to have time to be alone each day. She tactfully explained my need to grieve and think through all that had happened and all that I was facing. The next time Mathieu left my room, my mother handed me her cell phone with a number I readily recognized, dialed up, and waiting to be called.

"He left a message asking that you call him as soon as you have some private time. I'm going to leave the room now, too. I love you, Angie."

"I love you, too, Mom."

My hands shook as I touched "Call."

"Hello? Jared Lawson speaking."

"Jared, it's me, Ang..."

"Angie! I've waited forever for your call. Give me a second. I need to find a quiet place."

I could hear him running down a hallway, or some sort of hard floor, and then a door closed behind him.

"Angie, I am so sorry I did not get to see you before I left the hospital. I wanted to. Believe me, I wanted to. How are you doing? Are you OK?"

"No, I'm not OK. Why didn't you stop by? After all that we'd been through, you just left without saying goodbye? For days, I've laid in this bed waiting for you to come back. Then, I worried that maybe something was terribly wrong. The next thing I know, my mom tells me that you were discharged and on your way home. No, I'm not OK."

"Angie, the only thing more difficult than leaving you in the cave was walking out of that hospital without you."

"Well, at least you got to *walk* out!" I groused in the phone. Jared didn't respond immediately.

"I am so sorry, Angie. I wish there was some way I could have prevented that."

How I had missed the pure sincerity of his calming voice.

"It's not your fault. If it weren't for you, I wouldn't be here. How's Jarvis?"

"He's come out of it almost unscathed. In fact, I could conclude that the trip was actually good for him. I think he misses you, though."

"Well, I miss him, too."

"Angie, I'm sorry about the way this all ended. I really didn't have much choice."

"Of course you did, and you chose to leave without saying goodbye. By the way, Mathieu said you refused to cooperate during the rescue. Is that true?"

"Do you honestly believe that? I would die first before doing anything stupid to put you or Jarvis in jeopardy. I was killing myself to get back to you. I almost died out there before the search team found me at the bottom of the canyon."

"What happened, Jared?"

"I was told by some doctor that you were on your way to the hospital and that they were sending the second chopper up the canyon to pick up Jarvis. I was running back to the cave when I saw them airlifting Jarvis out. He wasn't moving or reacting. I knew something was wrong. I was looking up when I ran across some loose dirt and slid down forty or fifty feet? I don't know. My only option at that point was to try and make it to the canyon floor. I don't remember what happened immediately after that. There's a period of time that I can't recall. A team of park rangers on foot found me as I was trying to make my way back to the Lodge. The next thing I knew, I was in a helicopter and on my way to a trauma center in Las Vegas. That's when I remembered the doctor saying Las Vegas was where they had taken you."

"I didn't know all that. I'm so sorry, Jared. Are you going to be OK?"

"No. It's going to take awhile. Listen, Angie. I wanted to say goodbye, but there were photographers and reporters all over the place waiting to hear or see if we would reunite one last time. It was a zoo outside when we left. It wasn't fair to you, or Mathieu. As much as I wanted to see you, I knew I needed to step back and give you and Mathieu time. He was camped out in your room, for Christ's sake. I couldn't get near you without the world finding out or stepping into Mathieu's space."

"I am not Mathieu's space."

"You are his fiancée. I don't have the right to interfere. I really did want to say goodbye one last time, I just couldn't."

I could feel the tears welling up inside me. Was Jared letting me go?

We talked about the pain I was experiencing around my incisions. I told him how I would constantly think my leg was still there and of my phantom pain in places that no longer existed. I had medication to minimize and, hopefully, eliminate those sensations. I told Jared how much I hated the exercises I had to do twice daily and how rigorous they would be at Bryn Mawr.

"Will I see you guys again?"

"Maybe, if your hot shot 'husband' will allow it. But I doubt that's going to happen any time soon. Keep my number. If you need anything, you know you can call me. You know Jarvis would like to see you again, right?"

"Right."

"I will always remember you, Angie. I will never forget how brave and strong you were. I will never forget how patient and kind you were to Jarvis."

He was confusing me. On one hand he made me feel like our relationship was strictly forbidden. On the other, he asked me to save his number. How do you let go of something you were never quite sure you had in the first place? I appreciated his call and concern. We had shared life and death stakes, after all. We had said things in the height of our struggle to survive, but our conversation was different now.

Secretly, I knew there was nothing I could take to relieve the phantom pain I felt for Jared. We ended our conversation with me cautiously telling him of my regrets.

"Please don't take this the wrong way, because I am forever in your debt for saving my life. But I wished I had never gone to Zion. If I had continued on to Bryce, I would still have my leg. Now…"

"I'm so sorry, Angie. I wish you had gone on to Bryce, too, and that we could have reconnected some other way."

"That would have been nice. Who knows what would have happened?"

"Who knows?"

~

Despite my refusal to grant them an interview, the network news programs continued to carry our story. They persisted in sharing their versions of what had transpired between three people stranded in a cave, and how after their safe return, one stormed the other's hospital room declaring his love. Mathieu was portrayed as the unsuspecting fiancé. I could feel his hurt. Because of their absence from the video feeds, I could only assume that Jared and Jarvis declined interviews.

I learned that the final death toll was being set at 64 and that I would be the last to leave the hospital. Jared was the last person recovered alive. While our personal drama continued to receive national attention, it was disheartening how the media dropped the stories of heroic rescue efforts made by teams of people who put their lives on the line every day.

The day before we left for home, Mathieu took my hand in his.

"Are you ready to go home, Angel?"

"Yes. I'm really looking forward to sleeping in my own bed and eating home cooked meals. I need to see green grass and big billowy clouds. Rain! I want to hear it rain on the roof over my head."

"Well, you won't get to go home immediately."

"I know. But hopefully at Bryn Mawr I'll get to experience some of those things."

"Green grass? Yes. Billowy clouds? Yes. Rain? Perhaps. Home cooked meals? I can provide that. Your own bed? I can do better than that when they spring you," Mathieu said with a glint in his eye.

It was not the first time I had wondered what sex would be like as an amputee. (I still had trouble getting used to my new designation. My therapist said I should not shy away from it.) But each time I imagined it, Mathieu was not the man in my bed.

Mathieu's face fell and broke my silence.

"What is it, Angel?

We were seated facing each other. Mathieu was in a hospital chair, and I was in my wheelchair. Mathieu looked into my eyes. I held his gaze to make sure he would know the depth of my sincerity. In that moment, I knew I needed to be honest for both of us. I had a long road to crawl, walk, and run ahead of me. I had to start the long climb back.

MATHIEU

She needed time. She was taking drugs to prevent infection, inflammation, phantom pain, and depression. She had been through hell. She needed to reset and adjust to a whole new life. I had to accept her request for more space, much more space. She requested space and time without me. It felt like she was requesting a life without me.

"Mathieu, this is not about you. It's about me. I just need time away, to think things through." Those were her exact words when she left for the Grand Canyon. My body shuddered at the remembrance as she repeated them almost verbatim. "I need to take care of me," she continued.

"I could take care of you."

"That's just it, Mathieu. You would do just that. You would do everything for me. I would become totally dependent on you. I would be that baby that never learned to do anything for itself because its older brother or sister did it all for them. I need to learn what being an amputee means for me without your interference or influence. I need to do this on my own."

"Is the way I love you so bad?"

"Yes. I don't need to be smothered. I need room to cope. Coping means enduring the worst by accepting what I can't control, and working through what I can."

"I could learn."

"Don't you see? I have to learn first. I can't teach you when I'm trying to learn and adjust to everything myself. I'm going to make a lot of mistakes. I'm going to struggle: two steps forward and one to three steps back. I'm going to cry and get angry. If you're there to pick up all of my broken pieces, I'll never make progress and learn how to put myself back together."

She slipped my ring from her finger and handed it back to me. She was breaking off our engagement.

"I can't in all good conscience continue to wear this." She began sobbing as she placed the ring firmly into the hollow of my hand. "I'm so sorry."

"Angel, you don't have to do this. Please, keep it." I tried to offer it back to her.

"No. I can't."

It was the final blow to my severely wounded heart. She meant no harm or malice; of that I was certain. Angelica did not have a mean bone in her body. Sadly, that knowledge did nothing to minimize my pain. Angelica was strong and I knew she would emerge from her amputation and our break-up even stronger than before. Conversely, I knew that I would never recover. She had no choice in the loss of her leg, but she chose to cut me out of her future, at least for now. I tried to maintain a calm façade while inside I was dying.

"I am holding on to this ring, and when you're ready, come back for it. OK?"

Come back, Angelica. Please, come back...

ANGELICA

Mathieu lowered his head. He sighed deeply, and his shoulders shook. When he was ready, he abruptly looked up.

"Angel, I will always love you, always and forever. I will wait for you for as long as it takes. Hear me? In the meantime, I will give you all the space and time you need."

His combed his long fingers through my hair and gently cradled my head in his large hands. In a loving gesture, he brought our foreheads together, and we both started to cry. His tears fell onto the knee of his jeans.

"Oh, Angel, I want to be there for you. It's so hard to let go. Not now. Please, not now."

~

Mathieu did not let go easily. He did take a hotel room that night and limited his visits on my last day to a couple of hours in the morning and again in the afternoon until I was discharged. The Dufour family insisted on having my mom and me fly back in their private jet. A nurse accompanied us to the airport and made sure I boarded safely before saying goodbye. I would truly miss the wonderful caring staff at the hospital, but it was time to go. During takeoff, I took my mother's hand. I have never liked flying.

Leaving it somewhere below, I closed my eyes and said a final farewell to my leg. In some strange way, it felt like I was leaving someone I had known all my life, never to be seen again until I reached heaven. That was what Jared told me on the phone. He said that when I reached heaven, I would be whole again; I would have my leg. "No more crying, no more tears." *Easy for him to say.*

My mother smiled nervously and looked out her window. As soon as we reached cruising altitude, I was able to let go.

When I left home for the Grand Canyon, I felt as though my life was spinning out of control. Flying back home, many days later, miles above the earth, and in the Dufour jet with my mom and Mathieu, who was seated across the aisle, I realized that I had taken my life back in dramatic fashion. My trip out west had changed my life forever. *Always and forever...*

~

As the medical transport turned onto Paoli Pike, I breathed in the scent of harvested meadows and crisp fall air. A breeze blew through the trees that were beginning to drop their leaves as autumn made its approach to Chester County, Pennsylvania. We passed a community park bordered by a long scenic walking trail. I promised myself that I would one day walk that trail, and then I would run it. Sadly, I thought about the dance I would never have with Jared.

Breaking away from Mathieu was necessary, but not without anguish. However, I knew the ragged tear in my heart left by Jared would never heal cleanly. It was going to leave a deep scar.

CHAPTER EIGHTEEN

ANGIE

Continuing with my rehab at Bryn Mawr, I missed the first two months of school. I had received a prosthetic leg, and in October, I was finally cleared to move back home. I was slowly adjusting to life, as I would know it. Camille and my mother made themselves available to me, but spared me no mercy. They demanded that I take care of myself. No easy road for me. I had to do it all: vacuuming, laundry, shopping, doctor visits, and running errands. Every other night, Camille expected me to make dinner for both of us. It was exhausting. It was the best thing for me.

I went back to teaching in November and received a warm reception from my new students, parents, and fellow teachers. By the time Thanksgiving rolled around, three weeks later, I was bone tired, sore, and ready for a break.

No surprise, after the dinner hour on Thanksgiving night, Mathieu stopped by my parent's house. We sat quietly in the parlor and talked while dessert dishes were being cleared and cleaned. He looked good. I had to admit that I felt the same excited twinge I had the first time I met him. I was reduced to a blushing schoolgirl. He laughed and smiled easily. How I had missed his one-sided smirk. After our initial "How have you been?" he asked if I was seeing anyone. I had a strong feeling he was asking specifically about Jared.

"No. I haven't found a man that can keep up with me on the dance floor, yet."

"Oh, I think I'd like to try." He flashed that grin that always buckled my knees. "How about coming with me to our annual winter bash at the winery?" He reached for my hand. The touch of his skin sent a familiar tingle through my body.

So many times during my recovery and rehab I wanted to give in and call Mathieu knowing that he would rush in to take care of me. I knew with him I could surrender and find rest in his arms. He would save me from the hard work. He would have hired-help at my beck and call. I would not have to lift a finger. He would provide everything, everything except my need for self-worth.

"I don't think I can, Mathieu."

During the first week of December, the first substantial snow arrived in Southern Chester County. My students ran to the window and jumped for joy. I allowed them to watch for several minutes. They squealed as the snow became heavier and began covering the ground.

"OK everybody, get your coats on, we're going outside to play in the snow!"

My students and I ran around the playground and threw snowballs at each other. We made snow angels and did our best to build a snowman. The poor thing looked more like certain parts of the male anatomy, but they did not seem to notice or care. They were proud of their creation, and I had not laughed that hard since Jarvis thought Jesus should make the 911 call from the cave. I glanced toward the building and caught my principal looking out her window and laughing as well. I shrugged my shoulders and continued celebrating the day with my students. When they had had enough, I gathered them up, and we went back inside.

That night, I shared with Camille that I wanted to get away during Christmas break.

"Oooo! Where are we going?"

"We? Nowhere. Me? I think I'll spend the week between Christmas and New Year's in New York City. You know, take in a show or two, do some extravagant shopping, spend New Year's Eve in Times Square."

"You can't do Times Square on your own!"
Camille had a way of sounding frantic whenever she
disagreed with me.

"I'll be fine. Maybe I'll meet a tall dark handsome
man!"

"Angie," she scolded, "it's not like you to just go out
and pick up a stranger. Uh, at least not before the Grand
Canyon."

~

Much to the dismay of my parents and Camille, I left
for New York City the day after Christmas. I threatened to
never tell them about my travel plans again if they did not
stop hovering over me and trying to change my mind.

Camille dropped me off at Wilmington Station early
in the morning of the 26th. She wanted to come in and wait
with me, so I gave her that look that says, "Back off."
Camille kissed my cheek and said she would miss me while
I was gone.

I grabbed my travel bag from the trunk of her car
and waved goodbye. Leaving me on the curb, she
reluctantly drove away. Light snow was falling outside the
small magical train station. I had butterflies much like the
ones I felt when I left for Las Vegas. I grabbed the handle of
my new luggage and entered the station eager to start my
new life in a new year.

"Can I help you, pretty lady? Where might you be
going on this beautiful snowy day?" he asked.

While I surveyed his handsome face, he casually
took the handle of my travel case. I decided to play.

"To New York City for the holidays, and I fully expect
to have that dance you promised me."

We walked hand-in-hand to the platform to meet
our train. He was my Perseus and I would be his
Andromeda. For one glorious week we planned to dance
across the galaxies.

We promised Jarvis that we would meet him at Penn Station on December 31ˢᵗ, so he could celebrate New Year's Eve in Times Square with us.

Jarvis always knew how our story would end. Beginning New Years Day, he officially began calling me "Angie." He said that I would marry his brother and we would be together for eternity.

"Uh, let's not rush things, Jarvis..."

Jarvis was right. He was always right about many things. Together, the three of us made the long climb back.

If you enjoyed **"The Long Climb Back,"** consider reading
other novels written by Jill L Hicks.

"Will Power: A Romance Novel"
Will Power II: The Courtship"

Coming Soon:
"Will Power III: Pratt-i-cally Speaking"

ACKNOWLEDGEMENTS

First, I wish to thank my husband, Bill, who listens tirelessly as I explore various plot options and character introductions. I am forever thinking aloud. He has been my chief editor on all of my projects. Once again, he provided the beautiful cover design. Bill also set up a Facebook page for "Will Power" fans. Please join us on the adventure as we begin to work on the finale of my first series. Bill is the best!

I also wish to thank my sister Jane Niven, her husband, Mike Niven, a.k.a. "Monkey Mike," and my sister Joan Yarnall who once again proofed my second draft, identifying inconsistencies and grammatical errors. Thanks, guys!

I would like to offer another special thanks to Jane and Mike who were also courageous enough to travel out west with Bill and me. Thanks for inviting us along for the ride. It was the road trip of a lifetime!

None of these stories would have come to life without the encouragement of those who read the first book of the "Will Power" series and inspired me to continue with my newly discovered passion for writing. Thank you so much. The Will Power finale will be out soon!

ABOUT THE AUTHOR

Jill L Hicks was born and raised in West Chester, PA, and currently resides in Unionville, PA, with her husband, Bill. Together they have two daughters, Jamie and Jessie. Tragically, they lost Jamie, in an auto accident when she was just twenty. Jill also has a stepdaughter, Jenn.

Jill is very close to her extended family. She draws on her personal experiences and the stories of others to express the joys and sorrows of life and love.

Jill is a graduate of Penn State University with a degree in Music Education. In her spare time she loves to read, play piano, travel, ride her bike, sail, and spend quality beach time with her husband, family, and friends.

Ironically, Jill loathed reading until several years ago when she discovered the joy of relaxing on the beach with a good book. Pouring through 20-30 books in a season, she ran out of summer beach books to read and decided to write her own, ergo her first novel, "Will Power: A Romance Novel."

25502139R00126

Made in the USA
Charleston, SC
04 January 2014